A Spirited and Most Courageous Prince

Praise on Amazon for *Grant Me the Carving of My Name* and *Right Trusty and Well Beloved...* (the previous anthologies inspired by King Richard III)

'An inspired idea.'

'A mixture of the serious and the light-hearted, this anthology of Ricardian short stories is a must read.'

'A great compilation ... I love the idea that it is raising money for Scoliosis UK as well. A highly entertaining read.'

'Great book and brilliantly written.'

'What an enjoyable, entertaining, and (at times) heart-rending collection of short stories.'

'An excellent and entertaining series of short stories and poems. Some are exciting, some amusing, some tragic and will make you cry.'

'With a little something for everyone, this anthology delivers. I found the mix of genres very clever. Curl up with this book and enjoy a journey that will yield a rainbow of emotion and adventure. Well done to all the authors who contributed!'

A Spirited and Most Courageous Prince

An anthology of short fiction inspired by
King Richard III

With a foreword by
Robert Lindsay

Edited by
Alex Marchant

Sold in support of Scoliosis Support & Research

Also available:

Grant Me the Carving of My Name

Right Trusty and Well Beloved…

First published 2024 by Marchant Ventures

Copyright © 2024 the contributors

Editorial selection and introduction copyright © 2024 Alex Marchant

Further copies can be ordered from Alex at AlexMarchant84@gmail.com

The right of the contributors to be identified as the authors of this work has been asserted in accordance with the Copyright, Design and Patents Act, 1988.

All rights reserved. No part of this publications may be reproduced, stored in or introduced to a retrieval system, or transmitted, in any form or by any means, electronic, mechanical, photocopying, recording or otherwise, without the prior permission of the copyright holder.

ISBN: 9798338877654

Cover illustration: © 2024 Marion Moffatt at MadeMarionArt

To

the Richard III Society and all its members

for their efforts, big and small, since 1924 to restore
the good name of King Richard III

Contents

Foreword by *Robert Lindsay*	ix
Acknowledgements	xi
Introduction	13
Matthew Wansford, 1533 *Alex Marchant*	17
The Heads of Such Great Men *Kit Mareska*	21
An Indomitable Spirit *Wendy Johnson*	32
Looking for Anne *Judith Arnopp*	46
Borrowed Robes *Narrelle M. Harris*	62
The Banbury Road *Nancy Northcott*	70
There Will Be a Wedding *Brian Wainwright*	87
Lovell's Imaginary Boyl and the Mysterious Goat *Susan Lamb*	104
The Middleham Jewel *Joanne R. Larner*	111
Fotheringhay, 1476 *Matthew Lewis*	123
Confinement *Alex Marchant*	139
The Investiture *J. P. Reedman*	142
Watchers *Alex Marchant*	156
One Night in Coldridge *Alice Mitchell*	164
A Winter's Tale *Darren Harris*	170
A Middleham Fantasy *Bridget Beauchamp*	183
A Spirited and Most Courageous Prince… *Jennifer C. Wilson*	188

Foreword

Robert Lindsay

When I played King Richard III for the Royal Shakespeare Company in 1998, little did I realize it would start me on a road that would change my view of one of Shakespeare's most famous characters – and one of history's most controversial figures. Or that a decade and a half later I would attend that same man's funeral. My life on the stage has brought many memorable moments, but perhaps none stranger than that. Sitting in a packed cathedral, alongside royalty and fellow actors who had also played the role, to commemorate a king – dead more than five hundred years – whom Shakespeare depicted as a monstrous child-killer. Some people asked why we were celebrating this man.

With Elijah Moshinsky, my director for the RSC, I drew out the mischievous, comedic aspects of Shakespeare's Richard. Although the play is viewed as a tragedy, and the lead character as absolutely evil, this Richard III is a fantastic wit too, albeit a dangerous one. Shakespeare – with his profound insight into human nature – knew no one is a one-dimensional villain. And perhaps he was aware that the story of King Richard he'd been told was all lies – that his play was great drama but terrible history. Elijah certainly believed it was all Tudor propaganda, and our long discussions led me to question the truth. After the reburial I read more about this extraordinarily complex man, who, as well as being a talented military leader, passed such good, almost liberal laws.

The rediscovery of King Richard's grave reignited the debate over Shakespeare's – and traditional history's – portrayal of him. I think the world has finally realized it isn't an accurate reflection of the man, and books such as this are part of that development. In one of the stories, a mysterious visitor to Richard's tomb is corrected in his opinions by someone who knows the king's real history. And in another – an alternative history – a company of actors are rehearsing the play Shakespeare might actually have preferred to write. What would the real Shakespeare have written of the real Richard III if he hadn't been composing his plays during the reign of Elizabeth I – the granddaughter of Henry Tudor, the usurper who stole the last Plantagenet king's throne? And if there hadn't been a chance he'd have his head chopped off if he wrote the wrong thing?

The reburial of this young king, who was so besmirched by history and about whom such slanderous lies have lived on through the centuries, was an extraordinary and moving experience and I was glad to be a part of it. As I'm glad to be a part of this anthology which seeks to bring more of his real story to the public, while raising awareness and funds for Scoliosis Support and Research. After all the ridicule and Tudor propaganda, I hope that one day King Richard's reputation will be cleansed of all stains. And at least, now, he finally lies in state.

September 2024

Acknowledgements

We would like to thank all the contributors for generously donating their work to this anthology, including Marion Moffatt for her stunning image of 'Sir Thomas of Loxwood' used on the cover. (Prints are available to buy: please see details below.)

Very special thanks are owed to Robert Lindsay for kindly providing our Foreword.

Three stories have previously been published in some form and we would like to acknowledge permission to reproduce them here:

'An Indomitable Spirit' is an adaptation of four scenes from *The Traitor's Son* by Wendy Johnson, published by MadeGlobal (2024: ISBN 978-84-125953-7-6).

'Confinement' was originally published in *Yorkist Stories,* edited by Michèle Schindler.

'Watchers' was originally published in *Clamour and Mischief*, published by Clan Destine Press (2022).

About the cover artist

Marion Moffatt is an artist inspired by the natural world, primarily working in watercolours with mixed media elements. She also has a love of abstract art using the Earth and its flora and fauna as inspiration and Earth's minerals, such as amethyst, in the watercolour paints! A love of history also influences her – from medieval jousts and castles to Battle of Britain aircraft.

Originals, prints and greetings cards of Marion's art are available through her Etsy shop or direct from her.

Instagram: https://www.instagram.com/mademarionart/
Website: https://www.etsy.com/uk/shop/MadeMarionArt

Introduction

Six years ago, in 2018, a chat with fellow author Wendy Johnson about short stories we'd written about King Richard III led me to compile *Grant Me the Carving of My Name*, an anthology of stories by a group of similarly inspired international authors. Publication of that book led a year later to a second collection – *Right Trusty and Well Beloved...* – after we discovered many other authors likewise had stories about King Richard they felt needed to be told. Much has happened in the intervening years – great changes and upheavals in the lives of many of us. But one thing has remained constant, though it never ceases to delight me: readers requesting another anthology celebrating the life and times of King Richard.

Well, reader, don't say we haven't listened!

I'm thrilled once more to present a variety of stories by a superb company of authors – some of whom will be familiar from previous anthologies, others of whom have kindly joined us for the first time in contributing their work for a very worthwhile cause – Scoliosis Support and Research (formerly SAUK). Proceeds from the sales of these anthologies go to support the work of this charity that surely would have been close to King Richard's own heart, given what we learned from the rediscovery of his grave. In all three anthologies, stories touch on the king's own scoliosis, the lateral curvature of his spine – not, of course, a hunchback – which will have become generally known only after his body was displayed following the battle of Bosworth – and which formed the seed of lies about physical deformity that reached their nadir in William Shakespeare's play more than a century later.

Once again, the Bard of Avon is woven into more than one tale here. The writer who has done more damage to King Richard's reputation than any other over the centuries will perhaps always be in the sights of those seeking to restore that reputation. Some people defend Shakespeare's play, saying that King Richard, having reigned only two years, would be just a footnote to history without it; others might prefer it that way, if being a 'footnote' left intact the good reputation he enjoyed in his lifetime. After all, the Scottish ambassador (whose king was no friend of Richard's) said of him that 'Never has so much spirit or greater virtue reigned in such a small body,' while Dominic Mancini (also reporting to one of Richard's enemies) opined, 'The good reputation of his private life and public activities powerfully attracted the esteem of strangers.' Even the anonymous Crowland Chronicler, not known for his approval of the king, called him 'a spirited and most courageous prince', which provides the title for this anthology, as well as Jen Wilson's story.

But Shakespeare's depiction of Richard as the personification of utter evil has led many to question the veracity of the play, so perhaps, ultimately, it will help undo the destruction wreaked on his reputation by the earlier Tudor 'historians'. As the writer of our Foreword, award-winning Shakespearean actor Robert Lindsay, says, studying the play in preparation for performing the role prompted him to delve more deeply into King Richard's real story – and to conclude that the play 'was great drama but terrible history'. I have long admired Robert's work – both on television in shows such as *Sherwood*, *GBH* and *My Family*, and his many triumphs on the stage – but, like many Ricardians, I tend to avoid performances of Shakespeare's tragedy. So imagine my delight when, following his invitation to speak about the play during Channel 4's TV coverage of Richard's reburial, I heard Robert's spirited defence of King Richard and the revelation that performing the role had changed his mind about the real man. It's an honour that Robert has contributed our Foreword.

In this centenary year of the Richard III Society – of which many of our contributors are members – there is still much work to do towards fully restoring this maligned king's reputation. But it does feel as though in recent years the tide has been slowly turning, especially with the ongoing work by Philippa Langley and her colleagues in the Missing Princes Project. I hope this book will prove another small step in that process.

This book is dedicated to the many thousands of members of the Richard III Society (founded in 1924 as the Fellowship of the White Boar) who, for a hundred years and counting, have been working to bring about that change.

Alex Marchant
September 2024

Matthew Wansford, 1533

Alex Marchant

In February 2013, it was announced that 'beyond reasonable doubt', the grave of King Richard III had been found under a car park in Leicester, thanks primarily to the tireless efforts of Philippa Langley and the Looking for Richard Project team. As a Ricardian and writer of children's fiction, I realized this was my cue to write a novel for younger readers telling the real story of King Richard and his ascent to the throne. That story would be told through the adventures of a young page in Richard's service, Matthew Wansford, and so the 'Order of the White Boar' books were born.

The following is the very first part I wrote of Matt's story, a prologue looking back from his senior years, when a later king is embroiled in troubles of his own. The passage didn't make it into the final book, but I wanted to share this snapshot of the older man who knocked thunderously on my door that day in February, insisting I tell his story.

'Lies! All lies!'

Enraged, I tear the sheet of paper from the door of St Peter's church and rip it in two before she can stop me. She hushes me and, closing her fingers over mine, folds the pieces away out of sight. Her other hand grasps my elbow to draw me away from the church, but I shake it off. I see the fear in her eyes.

'Matthew, my love, come away. You don't know who may be listening.'

'I'm an old man – too old to be afraid any more. What can they do to me?'

Still she pulls at my arm, glancing all around. The street is busy, the cries of hawkers vying with the rumble of a passing wagon to drown out our voices. No one can hear us. But I let her lead me home. As she closes the door behind us, I glimpse something white flutter to the ground outside. I don't protest. It's one proclamation less in the city. And I know I can't destroy them all.

'Take a drink, husband. Come sit by the fire.'

Taking off her dusty cloak, she waves away the boy who has come to attend us and pours ale into a mug with her own hands. With a single look at my face, the boy scurries out of the room, leaving us alone.

'Drink, Matthew, and calm yourself.'

'Calm myself?' I stand my ground. 'In the face of these Tudor lies? Don't forget, we've heard these things before! Twenty-five years ago they said my lady Katherine had not truly wed Prince Arthur before he died, although we had all heard their marriage proclaimed. That meant King Henry could marry her as in God's eyes she was not his sister. Now these proclamations say that first marriage did happen, so the king can have his divorce!'

She says nothing. I know her affection for our gentle Spanish queen – and that all the women of the city feel Katherine is ill used by the king in his efforts to father a son. She doesn't deserve my anger, but still I thunder.

'Cromwell! More! Those lawyers! They argue and debate. They toss ideas around as though no real people will be hurt by them. One says a marriage is true, another that it was a sin. If the witnesses are dead, who can say what happened thirty years ago? The writers of history? Rewriters more like!'

After all, this isn't the first time. The names have changed of course – Vergil and Rous it had been then, writing their 'histories' under old King Henry, the seventh of that name. I've read them all. Every twisting of the truth was a stab inside me. But to how many others? How many now remember the truth of the old times, the days before that grasping Tudor usurper?

I am quiet now.

'You remember him?'

She knows instantly who I mean. I see her eyes soften.

'King Richard? Of course I do.'

How could she not? How could anyone who met him forget?

I remember. Almost fifty years ago, but I remember. As clear to me still as those lies nailed to the church door. As clear as the lies we have been fed in all the years since.

I was just a boy then, of course. But I remember. That day at Bosworth. Those days at Leicester.

When I heard the clash of battle, the screams of men and horses, the thunder of the traitor's troop as they surged forwards in the final moments. When I saw King Richard's battered, bleeding body flung over a horse's back and led past jeering crowds; the press of people in the streets, some turning away in sadness and disgust, while others thronged to support the victor. When I saw with horror his body hung up for all to gawp at. When I hid down an alley, afraid for my life, waiting for I knew not what. When I followed the good friars as they cut him down and carried him to his last resting place.

I had coins for them, and they let me – a boy only, no threat – enter their church. I held the stoup as they wrapped him in a shroud and sprinkled holy water. I sang his favoured *lauda* quietly as they lowered him into his swift-cut grave. They had had little time to prepare, they said – the new king had been impatient. Take him, dispose of him, let him be seen by living eyes no more, be no rallying point for rebels. But as we prayed together – before the earth was thrown in, the floor tiles relaid – I had a last glimpse of his face. Not the face of a saint, no, but neither that of a monster or a murderer. The face of a good man, a just man, I knew – and the face of a troubled man who had seen too much.

Three years before, life had been so different. Just three short years before, in that golden summer of 1482 ...

About the author

Alex Marchant was born and raised in the rolling Surrey downs, but, following stints as an archaeologist and in publishing in London and Gloucester, now lives surrounded by moors in King Richard III's northern heartland, not far from his beloved York and Middleham.

After timeslip novel *Time out of Time* won the 2012 Chapter One Children's Book Award, Alex began work on the 'Order of the White Boar' sequence, four books (so far) for readers aged 10+ telling the life and legacy of the real Richard III. Books 3 and 4 (*King in Waiting* and *Sons of York*) relate the story of the 'Dublin King', offering a theory which reviewers have called 'plausible', particularly in light of recent findings by the Missing Princes Project.

Alex is about to publish a standalone novel set in contemporary Scotland before starting work on a fifth 'White Boar' book.

Website: https://alexmarchantblog.wordpress.com
Amazon: https://www.amazon.co.uk/Alex-Marchant/e/B075JJKX8W/
Linktree: https://linktr.ee/alexmarchantauthor

The Heads of Such Great Men

Kit Mareska

Palace of Westminster, 1463

In addition to all his usual lord chamberlain responsibilities, today Will Hastings is sending invitations to the joust for Henry Beaufort, the newly restored duke of Somerset. Will also has to find a team to prepare the grounds along the river, choose the menu, and hire musicians, mummers, jugglers and other entertainers.

He has the easier day.

I must persuade my lady mother to be by my side as we honour Somerset.

Mother's position is much the same as Will's: invite Somerset to court if I must. But not so far into my life. Not as captain of my guard. And certainly not into my bed.

She is wearing pale green. That bodes well. I have learned to tread more carefully when she is cloaked in dark colours.

'I know you are convinced that this is what you have to do, Edward,' she says, as we sit on the couch and I have told her what I want. 'But why insist on my presence? Is it not enough that I remain in residence here while the man who killed my husband and my son is celebrated mere steps from my door?'

I don't bother to say that Somerset didn't kill them personally, that it was his army who did, while he was – how did he put it? *Curled up cramping on the floor of my tent like a shrimp ...* Dysentery will earn no softness of feeling from her. Their deaths at Wakefield carry his name, just as all those who perished at Towton carry mine.

'You are the highest lady in the kingdom, the one most suited to be by my side while I have no queen. Although, if you'd rather not,' I heave a sigh, staring towards the door, 'I could always send to the stews for a woman for the night.'

'You will not speak to me that way, Edward Plantagenet!'

Her voice is a miracle, an instrument that catapults me back to early youth. Even though I was jesting, and she knows it, still I suddenly have trouble meeting her eyes. The king of England mumbles an apology like a choirboy.

A quiet knock breaks my abashed silence. I'm grateful not only for the intrusion but for the authority that returns to my voice as I give the command to enter.

It's Dickon. Thank God. Maybe the presence of her youngest son, visiting from Middleham, will keep our mother from flaying me further. I wave him closer, but he studies Mother and me, as if sniffing the air between us, and after a quick bow, he drifts to look at one of the murals which give the Painted Chamber its name.

This is my fight, not a ten-year-old's.

'Mother, I know this is a lot I ask. I know how hard it was for me to welcome him to court. But I am just one person. I want to send a unified message to the realm, with my whole family behind it. I want George in attendance, too. And Dickon.' Who is definitely taller than when he left for Middleham. Every time we get together for visits like this, he'll be different. My future lord of the north is growing up without me.

Mother stares at me, iron refusal in the grey eyes. 'Your father and your brother died fighting Henry Beaufort. That, I could accept. I could even accept that, in his victory,' she blows a hard breath, 'that monster mounted their heads as trophies over Micklegate Bar. But to put a straw crown on your father? That is beyond bearing!'

'You knew about that? Both of you?'

Without tearing his attention from the painting of

Edward the Confessor's coronation, Dickon nods.

'But I tried so hard to keep that from you!' And I was glad I did, especially once Harry confessed to me that the straw hat had been his doing.

'I know you did, *Edouard.* Which is why you are not my sole source of information.'

She may have used the French endearment of my name, but this just became even harder. Time to fight dirty.

'"Get rid of all bitterness, rage and anger, brawling and slander, along with every form of malice. Be kind and compassionate to one another, forgiving each other, just as Christ God forgave you."'

Her right hand strays to her prayer beads, but her eyes remain dry.

'Of all the times I have longed to hear you recite the Holy Bible in that beauteous deep voice of yours, *this* is how you finally do it? As a weapon?'

'I am trying to meet you on your ground so that you will meet me on mine. This is important to me. And important to the future of our realm.'

Proud Cis never sighs. But this time, I see the effort it takes her to suppress it, the lifting of the straight shoulders, the thinning of her lips.

'Yes, Your Highness,' she says, letting me know it is the king, not the son, who has won. 'Who else will be by your side during this ostentation?'

I almost chuckle at her word choice. If King Henry had half the spirit of my lady mother, I would not be on the throne today. One does not laugh at Proud Cis, though. Especially when one has more news she will not enjoy.

'Well, there should be several hundred in attendance. On the dais with us, Lord and Lady Hastings.' I begin with them because she likes her niece Katey.

'Anthony, Lord Scales.' He, too, should be agreeable to her. Before he was beaten to death in 1460, Lord Scales' father-in-law was my godfather. And I'm hoping an open show of favour towards Lord Scales will further cement my friendship with the Widville family.

'The duke of Somerset, of course, will be with us as well, until it is his turn to joust.'

She only nods, having expected this.

'Then, lastly, there is the woman Somerset wishes to accompany him. Joan Hill. She is the mother of his son.'

'The mother of his son? Not his wife? You certainly have saved the least for last, Edward. Why have I heard nothing of this woman or the boy?'

'Charlie was born just after the battle at Northampton. Harry kept quiet about them to keep them safe.'

'Charlie. *Harry.* Her name, again?'

She remembers. She just doesn't like my calling Somerset by a nickname.

'Joan Hill.'

'And what is she that he does not marry her?'

'Mistress Hill is a seamstress.'

'So this seamstress is not good enough to marry a duke, but she is good enough to sit in the presence of the king of England and myself, who should have been queen?'

'She's good enough for me. I'm not sure about for you.'

A double failure. Mother will not be baited with humour or flattery.

'This is the first thing – the only thing – Somerset asked when I told him of this tourney. He's had little contact with her since the boy was born, wasn't always able even to send money. She has had to fend for herself and her son. He wants to make it up to her, bring her out of the shadows, if not to the altar.'

'No. I will not have my sons – my *younger* sons – in the presence of a fallen woman.'

She has countered a nearly fatherless boy with two truly fatherless boys. I should send her across the Channel to negotiate with France and Burgundy.

I am asking enough favours from her already, though. I take her hand, feeling thin bones beneath the soft skin.

'"You are the people of God; he loved you and chose you for his own. So then, you must clothe yourselves with compassion, kindness, humility, gentleness, and patience. Be tolerant with one another and forgive one another whenever any of you has a complaint against someone else. You must forgive one another just as the Lord has forgiven you."'

There – there it is, the sheen of mist over the stormy eyes.

'You came prepared,' she says, her voice no longer so tight.

'I know better than to face you otherwise.'

This time my smile is returned, if not in full.

'The rail,' says a quiet voice. Is it deeper than when he left for Middleham? He has crept up behind us, and we both turn to him.

'If George and I stand along the fence, we'll be part of the day but not part of the dais. And we'll be perfectly safe,' he adds, eyeing Mother. 'Would that serve?'

'Very well,' I say. Mother, more reluctantly, agrees.

'Do you think she actually can forgive the duke of Somerset?' Dickon asks as the door closes behind our departing mother.

'I don't know,' I admit. 'If she does, it will be because of God, not because of me.'

'And Father? Do you think he could have?'

Father's sincere blue gaze, his thrusting chin – they're here before me, in younger form. Will they, some day, develop the same stubbornness? The same sense of righteousness?

'I think he would have tried, if ordered to by the king. He participated in that stupid Love Day, after all. But deep in his private-most heart? No. Not for an instant.'

And you, Dickon?

It's right there, tickling my tongue, poking my lips.

I swallow it. If he cannot forgive, to say so would be defying his king.

*

I don't see it. Not at first. The woman by Somerset's side is rather plain. Instead of wearing a headdress as the other ladies on the dais do, she is in a simple linen hood, without any of the streaming tippets which are the fashion. It is lined with bright green silk, however, and its buttons are pearl. Somerset is trying to atone for her hardships.

Her gown and eyes are brown, as is what I can see of the hair within the hood. She looks, in truth, not entirely unlike Will's wife, though Mistress Hill's hair seems to be straight whereas Katey's is curly. And where there is a certain girlish spark to Katey, especially when she looks at Will, in Mistress Hill there is the quiet steadiness of a packhorse. At least Mother will not be able to accuse her of vulgarity.

Indeed, my lady mother is in full duchess mode, regal and cool to everyone, not just to Somerset's seamstress. She is dressed in charcoal and midnight, with touches of topaz to act as candles in the darkness.

Mistress Hill says little, though what she does say is appropriate. Somerset does not touch her, says nothing to her that could not be said before an archbishop. But his black eyes drink her in as though she were Helen of Troy.

'I must thank you, sire,' says Lord Scales, 'for allowing me to witness the joust before I depart for the north.'

Ah, yes. To Alnwick, with Warwick. Dear God, let them retake it and hold it this time.

'You mentioned that you and the duke of Somerset jousted once before?'

'Oh really, my lord?' Katey bubbles, as though in compensation for the silence of the other women. 'When was that?'

Scales shifts in his chair, brushes at his knee. 'It was ... when we were younger.'

Somerset displays none of Scales' reluctance. 'It was part of the Whitsuntide celebrations, Your Highness, in '56. We jousted before the king and queen.'

I smile. '1456. We were all Lancastrians then, weren't we?'

It visibly eases Lord Scales, though my mother frowns. She will not like that I made light of the vows I took to King Henry before God. And then broke.

'Who won, my lord?' asks Will. Hoping, no doubt, for an image of a battered and humbled Harry Beaufort.

'I did,' says Somerset. He glances at Scales and adds, 'It was a near thing.'

'His Grace is being kind,' says Scales. 'It was not close at all. I was eighteen and he schooled me. I'm hoping for another lesson today. Without the bruises.'

As the sun climbs, Somerset leaves to assume his armour. Katey talks with Mistress Hill about dresses and sewing, then about her son, Charlie, the warmth in her voice going beyond simple good manners and into fervour. Katey wants a son of her own so badly. I will have Mother speak to her; she and Father were married nearly ten years before their first child arrived.

Somerset trots on to the field atop the chestnut courser I gave him last week. For a moment, my eyes are on the splendour of the horse's red coat against the Beaufort blue and white. Somerset himself, though, has chosen to wear the tunic of my guard rather than his colours, the blazing sun over his heart. My gaze rises to his face, then higher.

He is in full harness. Where his sallet should be, however ... is a straw hat.

I buckle in laughter. Look at him again and

collapse over the arm of my throne. As I fight for breath and the muscles of my belly begin to plead, I realize that Somerset is taunting his remaining Yorkist opponents. *Those of you who would strike off my head? I'll make it easy for you, since you haven't been able to manage it thus far.* Despite the new rules that make jousting less likely to result in death, his message is not without considerable risk. Men still die.

I can feel my mother's disapproval, and even George turns wondering eyes on me from below, and I nearly regain control. Then I lose it with another peek, curling up again.

Like a shrimp.

I wipe my eyes and manage to right myself, striving for some sort of kingly dignity.

Seeing my composure restored, Somerset bows from atop his horse.

'Begging Your Most Noble Highness's pardon for my attire. But the sun is in my eyes.'

He is the one who is brilliant.

'Your Grace?'

Respectful. And so soft, I'm the only one to hear Dickon, who must have come on to the dais while I was doubled up.

'Yes, my lord of Gloucester?'

The formal greeting does little to mask the hilarity edging my voice.

'You like him. This isn't just … for peace. You *like* the Duke of Somerset.'

It finishes sobering me in an instant. Dickon may accept the necessities of politics. But this is personal. This, to him, is betrayal.

I can't explain to him now, here, that I understand. That I haven't been able to entirely shed the guilt that accompanies this new friendship. I can't tell him that, for all Somerset's arrogance and bravery by day, in the depth of most nights, Harry wakes screaming.

I'll have to talk to Dickon, and George too, about

this later. For now, all I can say is, 'I do.'

It comes out with the flat simplicity of honesty. And it looses a flurry of emotions on his face, crowned with the thrusting of his chin and a tight, single nod.

You weren't there, Dickon. You weren't at Towton. You didn't hear Will's teeth chattering so hard they rattled his visor.

You didn't step on what you thought was a corpse, only to have him grab your legs. You didn't hit the ground, sure that a dozen blades were about to pierce your flesh as though your steel plate were paper.

Arms leaden, head buzzing, wondering how much longer you could fight, only to see Somerset's hidden men come racing from the woods.

Rubbing your eyes, sure the Cock Beck was its usual brown and it was your exhaustion making it look red. Only to have the water not change back. And the crimson spread.

Bodies missing their ears or noses because men – your men – had collected them for trophies.

You weren't there, Dickon. For which I shall always be grateful. I do not want those visions living in you as they live in me. But Will Hastings was. Lord Scales was. The duke of Somerset was – and still is, many a night.

'Does the duke find death a laughing matter?' Scales demands of Mistress Hill as Somerset rides to his position. It is the first he has spoken to her beyond the initial greeting.

She possesses all the serenity I lost. Even the small mole at the left corner of her mouth does not quiver.

'Death comes to every one of us in the end, my lord. It is the duke's belief that such can be taken either as reason never to laugh or as reason to laugh all the more.'

'The defiance of laughter,' I say. A choice born more of anger than of happiness.

I beckon Mistress Hill to me. I want to keep her talking, to see what light she can shed on the darkness in

Somerset's soul. That doesn't stop me, though, from enjoying the way her front-lacing kirtle sways around her as she walks. She smells of honeysuckle and sun-dried sheets. I would like to lay myself out and wrap her around me.

She is no mere paramour, though, but the mother of his son. And somehow holy in her dignity. She means something to him, even if I do not yet understand the full meaning. An invitation could ruin everything.

She drops into a quick but smooth curtsey when she reaches me.

'About the straw hat, sire. The duke wanted me to be sure you knew … It is his apology. For Micklegate Bar. He said Your Grace would understand.'

My legs jerk. Mother does not gasp but she makes a sound that is close. And Dickon …

Dickon is silent. Much paler than a moment ago. Yet, his jaw retreats and his gaze softens as he looks from Somerset's mistress to where Somerset awaits my signal to charge.

We don't know, Dickon, none of us, what it may mean to move forward with Somerset as a friend. He is as unpredictable at court as at war. He put a straw crown on our dead father. Now he risks his life to put one on himself. And his seamstress, this clement, earth-eyed creature, has stabbed her needle into my heart in order to close one of its holes.

I will never touch her. Never ask. I am not Paris, to bring ruin to my city over a woman.

Peace has its hidden costs, as does war. No matter what they are, I shall pay them.

There must never be another Towton.

About the author

Kit Mareska lives in Colorado with her husband, their four cats and, on school holidays, their two daughters. When she isn't writing, she's exploring the Rocky Mountains and dreaming of her next research trip overseas. When she is writing, Kit is working on a Wars of the Roses series about the friendship between King Edward IV and William Lord Hastings, a trilogy about Lord Byron, and, most recently, a standalone novel about Lord Gilles de Rais.

Other short stories by Kit Mareska may be found in the following anthologies: *Right Trusty and Well Beloved…*, edited by Alex Marchant; *Yorkist Stories: A Collection of Short Stories about the Wars of the Roses*, edited by Michèle Schindler; and J. R. Larner's *The Road Less Travelled: Alternative Tales of the Wars of the Roses*.

Website: https://www.kitmareska.com/
Facebook: https://www.facebook.com/KitMareska

An Indomitable Spirit

Wendy Johnson

The following is an amalgamation of four scenes taken from Wendy Johnson's debut novel, The Traitor's Son, *readapted in short story form.*

Middleham Castle, Yorkshire, December 1465

Filthy and aching from weaponry practice, the bath forms a welcome prelude to supper in Warwick's chamber. Thomas Parr, quiet and purposeful, helps Richard from his grubby shirt, while Simon Kyngston sets to, hanging sheets around the tub and scenting the water.

Richard feels his cousin has been right about Tom. Six months his elder, the youth is proving a conscientious squire, and Simon has shown no manner of resentment at sharing his duties with him. In Richard's view that is only right: his brother George's boys compete for their master's favour, but for himself, he cannot hold with that. If squires fail to help each other, they're unlikely, in turn, to give good service to their master.

'Hurry, Tom, or the water will cool. I hate a tepid bath.'

With no response forthcoming, Richard glances over his shoulder, finds Parr shuffling from foot to foot, Kyngston quietly folding linens.

'Tom? If you can't untie my points, just say. I'm not too proud to fend for myself.'

Parr looks up, cherubic. 'Your Grace, forgive me, but I wondered whether you knew of your injury.'

'My injury?'

A curse as Kyngston drops a towel, apologizes. Parr looks to him for support, but the younger boy keeps his head down.

Considering the events of the practice yard, Richard tries to recall each blow, each thrust of blunt weaponry. Surely there can be nothing but bruises. 'You say there's a wound?'

'No wound, Your Grace.' Parr's voice wavers. 'What I mean is, your shoulder blade. Perhaps it's time to consult a surgeon.'

'A surgeon?' Flexing his shoulders, Richard makes exploratory circling motions. 'What are you talking about?'

Kyngston, casting the towels aside, joins Parr in a show of fellowship. 'Your Grace, this is not new, but I agree with Tom. It appears to be getting worse.'

Bewildered, Richard lashes out. 'So, whatever it is, you've noticed it before, but only now, when Tom points it out, do you choose to mention it?'

'Please, Lord Richard, I thought it impolite. As you never make reference to it yourself, I imagined you knew, but put no store by it.'

None of this makes sense, but Kyngston's face, scarlet against the flat yellow of his hair, reveals that neither he, nor his fellow, are lying.

A knot forms in Richard's belly. 'And you, Tom?'

'May it please Your Grace, I thought the same at first. I thought …'

'What? You thought what? Don't seek to keep anything from me, either of you.'

Kyngston kneels, as well he might, given his previous experience in the Clarence household and the durable sting of George's swift palm. 'My lord, I pray you, don't blame Tom. It was my duty to tell you, but it didn't seem right to speak of so personal a thing when you yourself made no mention. It seemed I would transgress. But Tom speaks true, your shoulder blade has sustained an injury in recent months. It looks … well, it looks wrong.'

Both can't be lying. 'Which side? Right or left?'

'The right, Your Grace.' Kyngston kneads his

bonnet between clumsy fists, while Parr fixes his master with a clear blue gaze, innocent as a chorister at Mass.

'Does it pain you, my lord?'

Impatient, Richard lets out a sigh. 'No, Tom. That's why I cannot understand what you're telling me.'

They do their best, fetch a looking glass and a smaller mirror of beaten metal, in the hope that between them he may catch sight of what they are compelled to reveal. But it's no good, a man cannot see the reflection of his own back, and if his shoulder is cast awry as they say, then the proof of it escapes him. Whatever the severity, it can only be conveyed to him second-hand. Exactly what he's always hated: reliance upon others to tell him the truth. Because, as he knows, sometimes they don't.

'The earl's physician is a good man,' Kyngston says. 'When my lord of Clarence suffered from stomach cramps, the earl sent the man across London to attend him. A plaster of anise and wormwood made up for the duke's belly, and the pain was gone by morning.'

Well-intentioned as he is, the boy is not helping.

'Tom, you say the shoulder blade looks out of place?'

'Yes, Your Grace. When you stoop.'

Richard gropes blindly, feels nothing but smooth skin pulled taut over bone: a shoulder blade like any other. But in bending forward, those same tentative fingers encounter a blade which rises up to greet them. So, it's true: something is amiss.

'Can we do aught to help you, sir?' Parr clasps his hands together as if initiating a prayer. Richard feels a sudden pity for him, for both of them: for their embarrassment, their awkwardness. Should they be revealing such a fact to George, they would be wearing the brand of his boot on their backsides.

He straightens, thanks them. 'No, but until I decide what to do, you must not speak of it to anyone. Swear it. Now.'

*

The earl has excelled himself over the Christmas season: plays and pageants, dancing and disguisings, wine from Bordeaux, oranges from Seville, and surreptitious gifts from the lap of French King Louis. Richard wonders about the festivities in London, and whether, during the York family gatherings and court masques, anyone is wondering about him.

His cousin's generosity, his warm invitations to ride out over the snow-covered hills, has prompted a decision, and on the Feast of Saint Sylvester, after supper, Richard dares to seek him out. Twitchy and tense, he ventures to the earl's inner chamber with its habitual scent of strewn herbs.

'Ah. What is it, Richard?'

Warwick is alone, merry and in good spirits, a gilt-edged volume open on his lap. He twists in his chair, face genial, open and peachy red in the glow from the fire.

Richard hesitates, sad and unwilling to blight his cousin's contentment. Guilt tugs at him, an unexpected sense of sorrow for the disappointment he is about to engender. What he intends to say may change Warwick's opinion of him forever. And the disenchantment, he thinks, will all be of my own making. He need in fact disclose nothing. He could stop now, before he begins; plead illness, tiredness, claim that whatever he intended to say, he no longer needs to.

'Come lad,' his cousin indicates the stool so often occupied by the countess, 'sit you down. I trust the king's letter has pleased you. The Garter is a prestigious order, and I agree with him that as your brother, George, is now a member, so should you be.' The smile is affectionate, genuine and elicits a brief rejoinder.

'The honour brings me much joy, Cousin.'

The earl's laughter draws a wet snort from one of his dogs. 'Well, I should not have guessed it by your demeanour, Richard. What ails you?'

Tell him. Just tell him and get it over.

'I need to ask you, Cousin … I've sustained an

injury. At least, I believe I have—'

'What manner of injury? I've heard nothing from your tutor.' The unruly brows have drawn together, deep creases scored between. 'Are you in pain?'

'No, that's the trouble. This doesn't pain me, but it should, surely.' Words spill from Richard's lips before he can present them in any coherent order. 'I can make no sense of it. I can't recall anything which could have caused it. I'm afraid the other boys may see, that anyone may see—'

Warwick holds up a hand, fingers splayed. 'Slow down. What injury? Where?'

Richard hesitates but realizes there is very little point. 'My back. Well, my shoulder blade. I know it isn't dislocated, but it is … damaged.'

'And how does your tutor believe this came about?'

'I haven't told him.'

'You make no sense, boy. If you have sustained any hurt, then your tutor should have knowledge of it.'

Richard is almost desperate now, wants for nothing more than to turn and run. 'I haven't told him, for I can't be sure the problem was sustained in the practice yard.'

'Where, then?'

'I cannot tell.'

Warwick's gaze is both intent and earnest. 'Might I see?'

Is this not why he came here? To have his cousin look and say, with his usual aplomb, that this is nothing, a minor inconvenience, something all boys suffer when they pick up a poleaxe and learn how to swing it.

'Richard?'

When he nods his agreement, Warwick leaps to his feet. Yanking the door wide, his cousin confronts the guards. 'No interruptions. You understand?'

A heavy thud, the click of the latch, the slap-slap of leather soles, and he returns: enquiring and expectant.

Richard rises, unlaces his doublet.

'Stop dithering, lad.'

Dragging the shirt over his head, Richard turns his back. Gooseflesh rising, he stares at the painted wall before him: at the bears, the griffins, the golden letter Ms for the Mother of God. He jumps at the touch of his cousin's hand, the pressure of his fingers, the skimming of rough palm over smooth skin.

Silence for what seems like an age, during which Warwick coughs but fails to utter a word. He realizes now how much he had wanted his cousin to deny it, craved reassurance that all was well, that whatever he thought ailed him didn't anymore. Well then, that being the case, his cousin must see the extent of it. Richard bends forward slowly.

The earl's considered breaths tell him all he needs to know. 'My physician in London. I think you should see him.'

Richard straightens. 'Then you agree, Cousin, it is an injury?'

'No. I believe it is a condition. One I've seen before.'

'Where?' Dressing, Richard emerges from billowing linen: a swimmer breaking the surface of water. 'Who?'

'A soldier I knew, fell at Saint Albans, one of my father's retainers. In his case, the spine had become crooked, one shoulder cast higher than the other.'

'And he fought? He could still fight?'

'Yes.' Warwick nods. 'The man was certainly not lacking in strength.'

Richard fastens his shirt with trembling hands. It seems unfair that his own body is playing him false, concealing its flaws, forcing him to rely upon the opinion of others.

'This man, he was a good soldier? He served my uncle of Salisbury well?'

'Indeed. And he was a man of good spirits,

accepted his lot. May I have your consent to speak to my London physician? The king wishes to see me with regard to my forthcoming embassy, so I'll leave for the capital in a week or two. As will you, for your formal investiture.'

Sucking his underlip, the earl calculates. 'What say we travel together? I could arrange for a physician to visit us. The man I've in mind is excellent, skilled in many things.'

Richard needs time to think. 'Cousin, I do not wish for the king to know.'

'You have your squires to attend you. Your brother will be none the wiser.'

'And George. I wouldn't care for George to know.'

The earl shrugs. 'The choice is yours to make. If you prefer to keep your own counsel, then I respect that. It shows tenacity.' Smiling, he lays an encouraging hand on Richard's shoulder. 'As for the physician, what do you say?'

'Thank you, Cousin. I shall see him.'

*

Unlike his York townhouse, Warwick's London home on Dowgate is entirely built of stone. Its expanse of garden, the beautifully arranged herber, after which it is named, provide a pleasant outlook from the window seat of the earl's private chamber. Had they visited in spring, Richard thinks, he should be gazing upon rows of colourful borders, a host of blossoming fruit trees. As it is, the only hint of green can be glimpsed among the box hedges: tough, spiky fronds piercing the layer of snow. He wonders how it is at Middleham, if Warwick's daughters have braved the weather, slithering over the frozen earth in their clumsy pattens, and whether Robert Percy is on hand to assist: an outstretched arm and a charming smile.

'Hurry, Roger. We need a good blaze.' Presenting his palms to the fire, Warwick nudges the bellows with a well-aimed kick.

The tousled-haired boy sets to work, bursts of ash and flakes of charred wood shooting upwards amid yellow flames. The physician is still downstairs, enjoying the earl's hospitality: warm bread and spiced wine for his trouble. Edward was right about Warwick's munificence. Their cousin's servants are the most envied in London; indeed Roger Fogge, still pumping the bellows, is well known to Richard. He used to light pricket candles at Shene, but L'Erber, he's told Richard, offers better pay – and its Calais-born pastrycook makes better pies.

Pointing his rump towards the growing flames, Warwick dismisses the boy.

'Doctor Brocas shall be with us anon, Richard. I'm to remain here during the examination. I trust you've no objection?'

'No,' Richard says. 'None.'

'You'll need to strip to the skin.' The earl shivers at the thought. 'I trust Roger has made good with the fire.'

A rap at the door and their visitor sweeps in; black hair, sallow skin, crimson gown bunched around his scrawny middle. The man has a smell about him, herbal compounds; sage and borage, the bright, cleansing scent of lavender. Tucked under his arm is an ancient, scuffed volume, which he places with obtrusive reverence on a side table.

'My lord of Gloucester,' the earl seems eager to proceed, 'this is Ralph Brocas. I have familiarized him with your problem. Doctor Brocas, I trust my cousin to your care.'

Warwick retreats to the hearth while Brocas scrutinizes his patient with dark, glassy eyes.

'The earl has indeed spoken with me, Your Grace, so I am aware to some extent of what is troubling you. However, I must consider the bodily humours in the first instance. So, how is your appetite?'

Richard is taken off guard. 'Reasonable, I suppose.'

Brocas blinks. 'Reasonable?'

Richard feels scrutinized already. 'I don't overeat.'

The glassy eyes narrow. 'I can see that. Do you sleep well?'

'Yes.'

'What of your dreams? Are they pleasant, unpleasant? Do they trouble you?'

Something prevents Richard from expressing the full truth. Blurred visions of his father still haunt him. Sometimes the duke is alive and happy: sometimes he is neither. Either way, it doesn't turn the dreams into nightmares.

'I do have dreams,' he says, 'but can barely recall them by morning.'

'Good. Would you care to disrobe?'

Richard shrugs out of his doublet and shirt, folds them, lays them aside, playing for time. He shivers, despite the raging fire, and Brocas circles him as you would a colt at Smithfield. Lifting Richard's arms, he peers at the clefts beneath, asks him to open his mouth, to show him his teeth. Yanking his hair, he peers at his scalp, looks into his eyes and pulls down their lower lids.

'A melancholic humour, I should say, the *Articella* is clear upon this. That said, there may be an excess of black bile, although such humours are unusual in the young.' Striding to the table the physician consults his tome. 'My lord earl, have your apothecary make up a tincture; valerian root is good, and yarrow. Make sure the duke eats plenty of meat when the days allow, stewed, or boiled in a soup. He may wish to avoid the more pungent of the spices, but basil, cumin and sage will do him good. Fennel too, again, in hot sauces or soups. Now, Your Grace, let me see your back.'

Richard does as he's bid; holds out his arms, raises them above his head. Finally, Brocas bids him lean forward.

'Lower. Then return to the standing position. Slowly, if you please, I must observe.'

Blood rushes to Richard's skull. Brocas bids him hold the position, while he examines his body from every conceivable angle.

'You may dress now.'

Straightening, Richard wriggles into his clothes, layers of linen and velvet serving as a refuge, a way of absorbing his shame.

'The condition is not entirely uncommon,' Brocas says, 'but its cause is unknown. The problem lies with the spine.'

'But does a person recover?' Richard speaks unbidden for the first time. 'Do things return to normal?'

Brocas sniffs. 'I'm afraid not, Your Grace. As a general rule the condition grows worse with time. At present your shoulders are aligned, but this will not always be the case. Eventually, as the spine becomes more affected, a discrepancy will occur.' He shrugs knowingly. 'But you're young, and measures can be taken, certain treatments. The body can be stretched, with ropes, to help straighten the spine, or exercises can be undertaken whereby the muscles may be strengthened. Sturdy muscle, so I've heard, can help the condition. Massage with certain oils can also assist.'

The earl strokes his chin. 'And what do you personally suggest?'

'As my lord is young, and the condition not far advanced, I would suggest he consider all of these possibilities. A strong body can resist the change, even if it cannot entirely prevent it.'

Warwick thanks the physician. They discuss his fee, arrange further consultations where urine will be considered and diet fully discussed, in an attempt to balance the patient's cold, dry humours. Brocas leaves and Richard retires to the window seat. He knew how it would feel once the condition was known, once it was out in the open, to be studied and stared at. At first, the problem had been his own, to consider or not, as it pleased him. Now it belongs to other people, to do with as they will.

Hitching up his gown, Warwick sits beside him. 'Well, what are your views? Are you prepared to submit yourself to the treatments he suggests?'

'I should need to learn more of them before I decide.' Richard makes a grab for his cousin's sleeve. 'If Edward knew about my injury, he would give up on me.'

'I think we've established that this is not an injury, but a condition.'

Do well, Richard, and come back to me a soldier. Richard recalls his final meeting with the king. Were Edward here now, would he still seek to encourage? Or would he divert his eyes, discouraged by the sight of his skinny, feeble brother?

Exhaling, Warwick rises to his feet. 'Well, I shall leave you to think about it.'

Richard's heart sinks as he struggles to judge whose disappointment would hurt him most: the king's, or that of the earl. He thinks he knows. 'Cousin, I hope you don't consider …'

'Don't consider what?'

He daren't even ask. 'The man you spoke of, sir – who fought at Saint Albans—'

The earl shifts his belt around his ample middle, adjusts his purse. 'What of him?'

'Did his fellows think him weak? Did they mock him?'

A sharp, pugnacious snort. 'I should've liked to see them try. He was a gristly bastard. Could have pitted himself against the best of them. In fact—'

There is a knock at the door, and a letter delivered, before the bearer shuffles out with apologetic speed. Heaving a sigh, Warwick breaks the seal and scans its content. 'I'm wanted at Westminster. If your brother asks of you, I shall tell him you send your greetings.'

'Thank you.'

The earl taps the parchment on his open palm. 'I suggest you consider Brocas' advice. We'll speak further when you feel ready.' Taking his leave, he lingers briefly on the threshold. 'Don't think this renders you in any way unworthy, boy.'

His cousin's pity, Richard decides, is harder to bear than any degree of disappointment. When the latch clatters into place, he returns to the window seat. Beyond the panes, the world is darkening as pale flakes dip and flutter.

His injury – his condition – is not transitory, he knows that now, but at least his father was spared the dismay. Gazing from the casement into a colourless infinity, it's as if he can see himself from a distance: a cowering insect, visible only to its Maker. Is this how he appears to the Almighty, when God casts down His eyes and seeks him out? A snivelling, shrinking, craven thing, fearful of his own shadow, and content to fail?

His cousin had tested him. At York, as they rode through the defences that once held their fathers' heads. And again, at Middleham, as traitors fell foul of the headsman's axe. He'd not failed those tests. Warwick had said so.

Clangs from Saint Mary Bothaw jolt him back to the present, and he decides that, just like Warwick, the Almighty has chosen to test him. Rising, he smooths his velvet, tightens his girdle, then squares his shoulders, as his cousin does.

He is a son of York, a scion of the house of Neville. If God trusts him to succeed, then he will.

*

Dusk is closing in, and at L'Erber servants touch tapers to wicks to chase away the gloom. The earl hunches over his writing desk. The candle at his elbow is dripping wax; glistening pools setting in opaque ovals upon ancient wood. He never ceases to work, sometimes far into the night: for the wealthiest man in London, the cost of beeswax can stand as no excuse. Richard knows he's working hard to narrow the gulf between England and

France. For now, Warwick tells him, is the perfect time. Duke Philip is sick and his son, the count of Charolais, is running affairs: restricting our merchandise, crippling our trade. Charolais, who has never been a true friend to Edward.

Sensing Richard's eyes on him, Warwick raises his head. 'Worried about the morrow?'

'I suppose I am.'

Throwing down his quill, his cousin straightens up. 'I take it you've come to a decision. What will you say to Brocas?'

'I don't know.'

Closing his eyes, Warwick presses thumb and forefinger into weary sockets. 'I fear you'll need to know by morning.'

'There's a lot to consider. The stretching—'

'Are you afraid?'

'No. Well, yes, I am.'

Warwick snorts. 'Good. I'd worry if you weren't.'

Richard acknowledges the jest, if indeed it was one, but finds he cannot laugh. His mind is fixed on his condition, or rather, on what to do next. He needs the earl's opinion but can't bring himself to ask. If Warwick were in my position, he thinks, he would know what to do, would have made up his mind before Brocas had even left the room. Edward likewise.

'Do you think this treatment – this stretching – would go on indefinitely, Cousin? Would I be required to submit to it for the rest of my days?'

Warwick leans back, chair creaking in protest. 'Only Brocas would have the answer to that. But if you wish to consider it, I can employ the best of physicians. I hear there are fine doctors at Montpellier, and I'm sure Monseigneur Le Roi would be happy to supply one. Louis is keen to incur my favour of late, and I would swear his man to absolute secrecy. If you prefer, I'm sure Brocas could recommend someone here, in London.'

If you wish to consider it: torture on a yearly,

monthly, weekly basis?

The earl places a hand on his arm. 'Richard, you may – not now, I grant you – but in time, you may wish to confide in your brother.'

'No. Not Edward. And certainly not George.'

'You don't trust them?' A mixture of sadness and curiosity, and again, that undeniable lick of pity.

'Not in this regard.' Richard surprises himself by the firmness of his conviction.

'Why?'

Surely it would seem obvious. George would see it as confirmation of all his suspicions, that he is weak and could never be his equal. Edward would be disappointed, for a while, but then he would find other roles for Richard to fulfil: a Garter knight who cannot wield a sword yet excels in matters of administration.

Richard compresses his lips. 'I need to prove myself first. When I've done so, they can make their own decisions about me, but not until.'

Warwick's face glows. Reaching across the desk, he squeezes Richard's hand. 'Well said, boy.'

About the author

Wendy Johnson is a long-term Ricardian. A founding member of Philippa Langley's Looking for Richard Project, she has lately assisted Yvonne Morley Chisholm's A Voice for Richard project. *The Traitor's Son* (MadeGlobal, 2024: ISBN 978-84-125953-7-6) is Wendy's debut novel and she is currently working on the sequel.

Books: https://www.amazon.co.uk/stores/Wendy-Johnson/author/B0D14SQJP3
Review: https://historicalnovelsociety.org/reviews/the-traitors-son/

Looking for Anne

Judith Arnopp

I am just nine years old when they send me north to be trained as a knight by the earl of Warwick. It is the first time I have travelled so far from home, and at first the terrain is alien and the accents quite foreign. Although I will admit it to no one, I long to return home. There are other boys there, boys who look at me askance on our first meeting. In the months since my brother was crowned I have found people are wary of approaching me since I am the youngest brother of Edward IV. I force myself to smile, to address them as equals for I desire no special treatment. I have already learned I can expect none from Warwick. On the journey north from Westminster, he reels off a list prohibiting me from many things.

'My household is vast,' he says. 'You will be a small tiddler in a very large pond, so don't look for any deference to be paid you. Here, you must forget you are a royal duke and behave like every other retainer.'

'Yes, my lord.'

It isn't as if I have grandiose manners, but he continues to harangue me, ticking off misdemeanours I am sure I would never think of committing had he not put the idea in my head. Chief among the strictures, it seems, are his daughters, although I can't imagine wishing to waste my time with them. Isabel is my age, but Anne is a mere infant, and furthermore, they are girls. I am not interested in girls.

In the weeks and months that follow, I glimpse them from a distance, but it is several years before I encounter Anne properly. I am on an errand, a message tucked safely in my sleeve, and we almost collide as she creeps backwards from the kitchen door with a bundle concealed beneath her cloak. She jumps and turns, her body freezing, her face stiff with shock until she realizes I am of no import. She scowls at me.

'Lady Anne.' I bow from the waist as I have been taught, expecting a genteel curtsey in return. Instead, she leans forward and waggles a finger beneath my nose.

'You must not tell, or I will be whipped. My nurse denied me any supper – I am hungry.'

I cast an eye at the hefty bundle of pies and pastries she carries.

'You must be if you are going to scoff all that,' I smile.

For a few moments we regard each other, like two pups unsure whether to bite or play. In the end, she relaxes.

'Here,' she says. 'You have it. I will get more.'

She thrusts her contraband into my hands, leaving me amazed as she hurries away, knowing full well that as her accomplice I am now as guilty as she.

Later, in my chambers, I wonder what manner of woman she will grow into. I unwrap the kerchief and find the game pie and fruit pastries crumbled together and rather fluffy. With a laugh, I feed it all to my dog.

*

Another few years pass before I encounter Anne again. I am riding back to Middleham from Warwick Castle with gifts and messages for the earl. It is early autumn, and the day is nearing its end; in a few hours it will be full dark. As the temperature drops, I draw my cloak about my neck and spur my horse on, eager to reach my destination before supper.

On the far side of the hill where the road drops down into a valley, I spy a group of riders a short distance ahead. Wary of footpads, I slow my mount and place a hand to my sword hilt, but on closer inspection I see the party is made up of women. It is unusual to find women travelling the road alone with no male escort. I urge my horse into a canter.

As I draw near, two of them notice my approach. They do not ride away but they shriek, struggling to control their agitated horses. The animals mill around, snorting and prancing, their panic made worse by their unsettled riders. The older woman, who is dressed as a servant, confronts me belligerently.

'We don't need any trouble from you,' she says, shaking her head and making her chins judder.

'Don't worry,' I say. 'I mean no harm.' I hold my hands up to demonstrate I am not in the mood for a fight.

'We have met with an accident,' the other one says. 'Please help us, sir.'

I peer through the darkening night into the face of a beautiful young woman. I recognize her at once.

'Lady Isabel? I am Richard of Gloucester. You know me, I think. What happened?'

Another figure rises from where she was crouched at the side of the road. I see now she is a mere girl. She wipes her hands on her skirts that are already mired. She also seems to have mislaid her veil and her hair is in tangles about her shoulders. Our eyes meet, and I see Anne recognizes me. She has grown, almost as tall as me now, her face no longer so plump, her figure beginning to blossom into womanhood.

'You must help me get him on his horse,' she orders without offering any greeting.

I look down at the fellow on the ground. He is unconscious, a trickle of scarlet running from his temple. As I dismount, I warily scan our surroundings. Anne squats down again.

I bend over the fellow. Poke him to see if he lives and jump when he groans loudly.

Anne looks up at me, brushes her hair from her face with the back of her dirty hand.

'What happened?' I repeat.

'A bird flew up and startled the horses. Ours bolted, but we managed to calm them. When we rode back, we found he had fallen off and, of course, he would strike his head on the only boulder for miles.'

She rolls her eyes impatiently. Tentatively, I touch his dressing and realize she has used one leg of her fine woollen hose as a makeshift bandage. A small leather boot is abandoned nearby.

'I think he will live, but he needs some attention. We must get him home.'

Taking him beneath the arms, I haul him upright and he hangs for a moment like a sack of wet grain. I am slight and have recently been experiencing pain in my back, so it is with great difficulty that I manage to manoeuvre him into the saddle. Anne helps me bind him in place to stop him slipping off again.

'Thank you.' She smiles suddenly, her face lighting up, intelligent and confident, ready for anything. 'I remember you. I'm afraid I have no dainties with which to bribe you this time.'

Taken aback by her rude humour, it is a few moments before I realize she is waiting for me to help her on to her mount. Belatedly, I link my fingers, forming a stirrup for her muddy, naked foot. I hoist her into the saddle.

'Oh, I nearly forgot my boot. Can you pass it up to me?'

*

Once I am settled in at the castle and have passed on my messages, I join the family for supper in the great hall. My old companions are there – Lovell and Ratcliffe. While we partake of supper, we spar and share memories, our voices growing louder as our excitement increases. I lean back in my chair, listening to far-fetched stories, when someone insinuates themselves between Lovell and me. An arm reaches across the table and steals a honeyed wafer from my plate.

'Hey!' Instinctively, I grab the wrist, noticing too late that the hand of the thief is as small as a child's, the wrist as slim as a girl's. I look up into the face of Anne Neville and release her as if I have been scalded.

My cheeks flame.

'Forgive me, Lady Anne. I thought it was one of the …' I indicate my companions but find they have moved away, leaving me alone with her.

'I know what you thought,' she says, dropping beside me on to the bench and taking an enormous bite of my pastry. Honey drips down her chin and she scoops it up with her finger, licks it, rolling her eyes as if in ecstasy.

'Thank you for saving us today,' she says with her mouth full. I try not to stare at the crumbs clinging to her lips. 'Isabel says you were our knight in shining armour, like Lancelot to the rescue.' She holds an imaginary sword aloft and I laugh, uncertain if she mocks me or not.

'It was my pleasure, lady. An unlooked-for relief from the tedium of the ride. Did your man recover?'

'Oh.' She swallows her food, her tongue straying around her teeth in search of lost morsels. 'He will, but he is making a great deal of fuss about it. I am told he will soon be as good as new, but he owes the thanks to you. I would never have been able to haul him on to his horse. We might still be out there had you not happened along just at the right moment – as if sent by angels.'

She clasps her hands in a parody of prayer and turns her eyes heavenward. Now I know she is mocking me. I laugh properly this time, and thus encouraged, she turns again to my plate and helps herself to a second wafer.

'Where have you been during all the recent upheavals? Have you met Edward's new queen?'

'Yes, I saw her.' 'What do you think of her? Is she as beautiful as they say?'

'I am no judge of beauty. She is very … well, she

attracts the eye, but I feel she lacks something. In conversation she is dismissive and cold ... when speaking to me, at least.'

Anne leans forward, interest in her eye.

'Are you jealous?'

'No! I am too young yet to consider a wife.'

'No, no!' Her laugh rings out again. 'I mean, are you jealous of the demands she places on your brother. Father says you are really close. Does the king still make time for you?'

Not so as you'd notice. I do not answer aloud; I shake my head and try to deflect her. In truth, I am disenchanted with Edward's choice of bride, and I know Warwick is too. While the earl was busy making arrangements for a diplomatic foreign union, Edward married Elizabeth Woodville behind his back – a commoner, a Lancastrian widow and mother of two sons. I am not sure which crime is worse. I have not yet forgotten the earl's fury when he learned of it.

If it were only Elizabeth we had to deal with, it wouldn't be as bad, but she has a vast family, all seeking positions at court, looking to increase their riches and power. They are loud, demanding, and I am glad my duties in the north spare me the necessity of attending court regularly.

Anne turns the conversation to other, lighter things. She tells me of her dog, Troy, and her favourite horse, and belatedly asks about my own. As we converse, I crack and shell nuts, dropping the choicest of them into her waiting palm, watching and enjoying the pleasure with which she consumes them. It is as if we are the only two in the crowded hall, as if the musicians have stopped playing and the dancers turned to stone. I am captivated by her manner, for I have never encountered a girl like her. She is free and relaxed, and where I am usually tongue-tied, she makes it easy for me to find a reply. The conversation does not run dry as it usually does. Anne helps me to find myself.

We are in mid-conversation when a small dog leaps on to her lap. She abandons her sentence and the spell between us is broken. We straighten up, draw apart and become aware of the company. I blink and look about the hall, and the first face I encounter is that of the earl of Warwick. He is clearly displeased. My heart quails. He has been watching me, watching Anne – the daughter he ordered me not to dally with.

But this is not mere dalliance.

After that night I cannot stop thinking of her. I make the decision to ask Edward for her hand. She is a good match, of noble blood and her dowry a rich enough lure for any man. Her father can find no fault in a marriage to a royal duke, the brother of the king. If they feel she is too young, I don't mind waiting.

For the first time I imagine myself with a wife. I can picture returning home to her when my work is done. I can see our children, strong boys, and girls all made in Anne's image, a family such as I have never really known. She was made for me, I know it.

But, before I can approach the king to beg his permission for the match, Warwick has grown tired of pandering to the Woodville queen and betrays the king. I am astounded when I learn he has agreed a truce with Marguerite of Anjou and used the lure of Isabel's hand to tempt my brother George, duke of Clarence, to join them. His plan is to oust Edward from the throne and reinstate Henry VI, and furthermore, just to honey George's pudding, he promises to make him Henry's heir.

And Anne, *my Anne*, becomes a gaming piece. She is used to broker Warwick's truce with Marguerite and sold in wedlock to her son, Edward of Lancaster. I cannot sleep knowing Anne is overseas, in a foreign land, in another man's bed.

I think of Anne often as I follow in King Edward's wake, joining him in exile, offering unwavering support to his cause, fighting in battles against men I'd once called friends. I look for her everywhere, yearn for just a glimpse of her face. I focus on the things she said, the jokes we shared, the strange unbidden understanding that blossomed so suddenly between us. I cannot accept she is now another man's wife on the opposite side of the war we fight. By definition, she is now my enemy, yet I know if I were to see her, I would open my arms and hope she'd fall into them.

War is always an ugly thing, but it is uglier still when kin fights kin. Warwick is the son of my mother's brother. After I lost my own father, I looked to Warwick to take his place. George is my brother; awkward and argumentative he may be, but sprung from the same womb, we can never really be foe. So, when Edward asks me to accompany him, and we somehow manage to persuade George back to our side, I celebrate that the brothers of York are reunited.

When I next encounter Isabel, I besiege her with questions, but she is unable to answer most of them. She reveals enough for me to realize that Anne is not happy. Anne finds no favour in Edward of Lancaster and evidently, he finds little joy in her. I try to imagine her forced to act against her will. She will not make life easy for a husband not of her choosing, and I pray Lancaster is not unkind.

*

A great battle is fought at Barnet, and afterwards I learn that Warwick has been slain. After his crimes against my brother, I shouldn't weep for him but I do. Not just for his death but for everything that went before. I shut myself away and pray his soul will not linger too long in purgatory. Anne will have heard the news and will be grieving, and my fear for her grows, for she is now at the sole mercy of her husband ... and Marguerite.

Another battle looms, this time near the abbey at Tewkesbury. I learn that Marguerite is awaiting the outcome at a nearby priory. I imagine Anne is with her, for

Edward of Lancaster fights in this battle too. I brood as I am helped into my armour, my sword placed in my hand. When the battle commences, as I wield my sword, I watch for him and when I glimpse his colours, I work my way in his direction. My blade slices Lancastrian flesh and breaks Lancastrian bone, sheds Lancastrian blood. When we come face to face, we both pause, raise the visors of our helmets.

'Gloucester,' he snarls.

He is taller than I – most men are – but he is not as strong, not as well-trained, and he lacks my fury. My grip tightens on the sword hilt, and we begin to circle. White boar and golden lion cub. He knows I want to kill him and he knows the reason why. He conceals his fear as we move closer, swords raised. The clamour of battle drifts away until it seems I am alone with Lancaster on the blood-drenched plain.

His mouth moves, his words lash me.

'The first time I took her, she tried to fight me,' he says, his mouth squared and ugly. 'But she came to like it, after a while.'

Anger and envy rage through my body, my heart cries out for vengeance, and my arm is empowered by his crimes. When I make the killing blow, I am glad.

*

With the battle over, as soon as the blood has dried and our wounds are healing, I seek an audience with the king.

'Why so formal, little brother?' he laughs when I greet him with a bow, but I do not relax. I cannot smile and laugh and congratulate him on our great victory while Anne remains in peril. If I do not persuade him to grant me her hand now, it may never happen. I look into his puzzled eyes.

'You promised me a boon.'

'I did, little brother. After the way you have fought these past months, you can have anything that is within my power to give.'

'Lancaster's widow.'

'Ah, yes, the lady Anne. She is yours, whether she will have you or not.' He waves a hand in the air, as if he is holding a wand, granting wishes.

I bite back an ugly response and bow again. 'I thank you, Your Majesty. Do you know her whereabouts?'

'She was taken into custody with the Anjou woman, but knowing she was given little choice in her actions against us, I spared her punishment. Having finally rid ourselves of adversaries, we must hope she doesn't carry Lancaster's heir. I believe she is with George and her sister.'

'At Erber House?'

'I imagine so. Now, join me for supper, Richard. There is much for us to discuss.'

I shuffle my feet, reluctant to tarry. But he is the king. So I join him, listen to his unsubtle jubilation at winning back his throne and ridding himself of enemies. He has no remorse, no inkling that Warwick's outrage may have been justified. As I chew without tasting, my mind drifts off, only brought back to the present when he leans forward and reaches out to lightly touch my arm.

'Richard, you know the old king had to die? You know I had no choice?'

I nod once, discomforted but understanding the necessity of removing the old king. Edward has given Henry a martyr's crown. Marguerite will be furious when she learns of it but, held fast in the Tower, she is powerless, with nothing left to fight for, now her son and king are dead.

*

In the morning, I rise early and ride to Erber House where George is in residence. I am expecting a squabble, for he has never been one to enjoy another's reward. If I must fight him for Anne, then so be it. I am expecting trouble but not the hostility with which he greets me. Before I have dismounted or opened my mouth to speak, he appears on the threshold and refuses me entry.

'We are busy. You must call back in a week or two.'

'The king has promised me Anne's hand. I wish to see her.'

He blocks the doorway.

'She is not here.'

I sigh. I know he lies. You'd think from the practice he's had, George would be skilled at deceit, but he is a poor liar, and always has been. He just doesn't seem to care his deception is transparently obvious. I cling to my temper.

'Come on, George. Let me see her.'

He comes threateningly close.

'How many times do I have to tell you? She is not here; she has left us. I don't know where. Perhaps she has gone to Beaulieu to be with her mother.'

'Very unlikely, George. This is Anne we are speaking of. She would never just leave without telling you her direction. Isabel will know. Let me speak to her.'

While George fumbles for an answer, I look at the ground, idly striking my thigh with my gauntlet. Then I look up. 'I'm waiting, George.'

'Isabel is not well. You can't see her. I will speak to her on your behalf and send you word later.'

I lean closer, my voice abrasive with rage.

'You're a bad liar, George, you always have been. Have you learned nothing in the past few years? Don't you owe me? Have you forgotten how, after your betrayal, I spoke out in your defence and protected you from the stain of treason? You betrayed our brother, your king, and now you are betraying me by denying my right to speak to Anne. You are a blemish upon the house of Plantagenet.'

Knowing it is useless, I turn towards my horse, and once remounted, I shout across the bailey.

'I will see Anne, George, even if I have to bring

the king with me to enforce it. In the meantime, ensure she is well cared for or you will answer to me. I won't give up, George. I do mean to make her my wife.'

I ride back to Westminster, take my worries to the king, but I am foolish. I should have battered down George's door and taken Anne from him while I had the chance. In the intervening days she disappears and I am at a loss, not knowing where to begin my search.

I question George, but he remains obdurate. Even when Edward demands he reveal her location, he pleads ignorance. I make enquiry of his wife, his servants. I question his friends, I question his enemies. I seek out Anne's friends. I visit her mother in sanctuary at Beaulieu Abbey. Nobody can tell me her whereabouts. It is as if she has been spirited away.

But I will not give up.

*

Months pass. I grow weary of searching, despairing she will ever be found. I have lost her, but I cannot rest. Each time I close my eyes, I see her in chains in the bowels of a filthy ship, taken overseas, sold as a slave. I see her locked in a tower, hungry, ragged and cold. I see her in a filthy brothel, ill-used, abused, ruined. Abandoning sleep, I rise and saddle my horse, ride through the streets of London. For the first time since Tewkesbury, I am out of ideas. I am merely riding aimlessly, for want of something better to do. In the end, tired and hungry, I stop at a lowly inn, slump at a grubby table and order a cup of ale.

It is the haunt of thieves and ne'er-do-wells, but when they eye my finery, I do not fear them. I may carry a purse fat enough to tempt them, but I also have my sword. After a while they lose interest in me and resume their game of dice, their conversation floating unheeded about my head. But then, one word stands out from the rest. A name. A name I know: *Clarence.*

I raise my face from my cup, turn surreptitiously

towards them, waiting for the name to crop up again.

They are discussing the women at another inn. Most it seems are generous with their charms, but one, a recent arrival, refuses. Apparently, she emptied a jug of ale over the head of a would-be suitor, causing great hilarity among the brethren. I drain my cup and move across to their table where I slap a few coins before them, keeping them covered with my hand.

'Tell me the name of the inn you speak of, and the coin is yours.'

The men eye the sovereigns, just visible through my fingers. One of them draws the back of his hand across his nose and leers in the approximation of a smile.

'Maybe the information we 'ave will cost you more'n that.'

I curl my lip.

'Perhaps you'd prefer the point of my sword. I could cut the information from you before I take your tongue.'

He backs down. 'All right, all right, no need to get shirty. One of the inns in Southwark, the cook house at the back of the Cock.'

I remove my hand and he snatches up the money.

'If I discover you have lied, I will return. Watch yourself.'

Dragging my reluctant horse's nose from a bucket of oats, I mount and urge him towards London bridge. By the time I near my destination, an early sun is bringing out hawkers, shoppers, prostitutes, preachers, runaway brats. The clamour is loud.

'Make way, make way!' I call, wishing I'd brought a few retainers along to clear a path. In the end I resort to my whip and, laying about those in my way, I fight a passage through.

The stench of the Thames rises, the sharp tang of urine and worse. A woman screams abuse at me, her partner dragging her away from the reach of my whip. I pay them no mind. My only intention is to cross the bridge to the murky streets of the south bank.

Southwark is the haunt of thieves and whores, but at this time of day it is quieter than the bridge. It is as night falls that the streets will fill with those in search of mischief. My heart quails at the thought of Anne in such a place, yet I pray to God she is here and I find her unscathed.

The Cock Inn lies towards the end of this street. I turn into the courtyard, rein in my horse. Before dismounting, I assess the surroundings and, keeping hold of my whip, I slide from the saddle and flip my cloak behind me to allow ease of access to my sword. Stepping over piles of refuse, I approach the door and, since it is so early, the inn is almost empty when I enter.

I order refreshment, looking around as I make light conversation with the innkeeper. His responses are surly, unforthcoming. I move to a table near the grimy window, where a cat snakes around my ankles as I sip my ale, considering my next move. If I ask the landlord whether he is holding Lady Anne Neville prisoner, he is not likely to make an honest reply. I need to ask a pot boy, or someone eager to earn a coin. There are no servants in this chamber, but I hear voices from below, the clash of pans indicating the location of the kitchen. When the innkeeper bends down to examine his barrels, I take my chance, put down my cup and, almost tripping over the cat, make my way stealthily to the stairs. They creak as I descend. I am halfway down when a young boy confronts me.

'Yer in the wrong place, mister. This 'ere is the kitchen, guest quarters is upstairs.'

'I am looking for a girl.'

An older servant comes forward, rubbing his hands on a soiled cloth, a look of amusement on his face.

'The girls are upstairs too, sir. There's nothing for you down here.'

I should have chosen my words more carefully.

'I am not seeking a whore. I am in search of a

particular woman, a lady by the name of Anne Neville.'

A burst of laughter issues from the group of servants now clustered at the foot of the stair, their faces raised, red with perspiration from their labours over hot pots and fires.

'I am the Lady Anne.' One of the girls gives a mock curtsey. 'And this 'ere is my friend, the queen o' England.'

I do not smile. I tighten my lips, take a deep breath.

'I have been informed that a young woman is being held here against her will. She is ... different from the women around here. She is refined, a lady ... you will have noticed her.'

One of the women shuffles her feet, lifts her chin to speak.

'D'you offer a reward, sir?'

There is something in her face that gives me a breath of hope, but I conceal my eagerness.

'Yes, of course, if you help me find her.'

The servants murmur. The woman glances to the top of the stair, puts a finger to her lips and beckons me forward. As I follow, it occurs to me it could be a trap. They could knock me on the head and steal my money. My horse outside is worth a year of their wages alone.

She draws back a bolt and creaks the door open, and abandoning caution, I step inside. She follows at my heel.

As my eyes grow accustomed to the lack of light, I make out the hump of a sleeping figure on a squalid mattress.

'The master locked her in 'ere because she gave him lip. She's useless in the kitchen and was rude to the customers. I knew she didn't belong 'ere, but I never guessed she was a lady. I never knew she was important.'

I step closer. The figure on the mattress rolls over and pulls herself upright. Her clothes are ragged, her limbs are bruised, and she has an angry-looking burn on her forearm. Her hair hangs in tangles about a dirty face, a face that is thin and ill-nourished yet not devoid of strength. She holds out a filthy hand and dazedly I take it, pull her to her feet and look into her red-rimmed eyes. She tosses her head, her eyes glistening with what could be fever, or could be tears.

'Well, it took you long enough to find me,' Anne says. 'And your damned brother George has a lot to answer for.'

About the author

Judith Arnopp, lifelong history enthusiast and avid reader, holds an English/Creative Writing BA and Medieval Studies MA and lives on the coast of west Wales where she writes both fiction and non-fiction. She is best known for novels set in the medieval and Tudor period, such as *The Beaufort Chronicle*, *The Kiss of the Concubine* and *The Henrician Chronicle*, taking the perspective of historical women and more recently, of Henry VIII.

Judith is a founder member of re-enactment group The Fyne Companye of Cambria, which is when and why she began sewing historical garments, leading to publication of *How to Dress like a Tudor* (Pen & Sword, 2023). She also runs a seaside holiday let in Aberporth and when she has time for fun, gardens and restores antique dolls and dolls houses. Her new novel is *Marguerite: Hell Hath No Fury* (coming soon).

Website:	www.judithmarnopp.com
Books:	author.to/juditharnoppbooks
Blog:	www.juditharnoppnovelist.blogspot.co.uk/

Borrowed Robes

Narrelle M. Harris

Zigmund Berger adjusted the rubberized breastplate on his chest a third time, cursing the damned thing.

'Hold still, Zig,' muttered Vikram Singh, trying to adjust the buckle. 'I just need to …' The wardrobe assistant managed to loosen it a notch and then straightened up and checked his mulberry-coloured turban hadn't begun to unravel while he was bent over. 'Try that.'

'Now it's too loose.'

'Suck it up,' laughed Zig's cast mate, Chris Almeida. 'Let the discomfort feed into your character. Henry's all cranky in these scenes anyway.'

'Fine. Let's get on. Where were we?'

'*I fear the sun* …' prompted Chris.

Zig cleared his throat and changed his stance, transforming suddenly from irritated actor to frustrated wannabe king.

'I fear the sun will not be seen today; this louring sky portends defeat,' said the pale Henry Tudor, his eyes darting heavenward in concern. 'As likewise, all my labours bent to gather close those vanished sons of York, in vain, undo my mother's schemes.'

'Bestir you not, my lord, in fear,' said Chris as William, his burly companion. 'For my agents spread abroad a tale of vile treachery, an uncle's bloody deed.'

'How now?'

'A murder most unnatural!'

'Sweet William, my thanks for this report, sung so sweetly to mine ear. Our lies will make a princely bed and grave for those sweet babes to lie in, when once I have them in ambition's grip … ugh, hang on. Sorry, sorry.' Zig tugged at the breastplate that had ridden up his torso and now pressed uncomfortably into his neck. 'Vikram, I absolutely cannot act like this!

Vikram dashed out from the wings to untie it.

'Stop tugging it! You're changing the shape of it.'

'Can we move the buckle?'

'I can do that,' Vikram agreed patiently. 'Come backstage at the end of the day and I'll remeasure. I think I can use some Velcro and fasten it to your trousers.'

'God, anything.'

'Do you need it for the scene at all, Zig?' asked Chris. 'Everyone knows Henry loitered on a hill until the last minute, and even then he tried to hide in the middle of his mercenaries. Not like King Richard, leading the fray.'

Zig straightened his doublet. 'You make him sound like a complete coward, Chris. Bad enough Shakespeare writes him as a whiny, spineless little traitor.'

'That's because he was a whiny, spineless little traitor. And a mummy's boy. And he plotted to kill kids …'

'He never.'

'So King Richard spread his own rumours and then, ta-daaa, produced Edward and Richard after the battle as, what, a surprise for their mum? An April Fool's joke in August?'

'Chris, my job is to get into his head, and every villain is the hero of their own story, yeah? Besides, history is a little unclear about how those rumours got spread.'

'Well, the boys showed up again from Burgundy a month later, so (a) not dead; (b) Richard would hardly spread rumours against himself; and (c) if it wasn't Henry, it was probably those bloody Stanleys.'

Vikram had fiddled with the straps and now offered the breastplate up for Zig to try it again.

'Does it need to be remoulded?' asked Vita Carvalho, the director, coming up to the foot of the stage. 'We can't have it coming loose or doing you an injury in the swordfight. It has to hold up five nights a week and matinees on the weekend.'

'I have to hold up, you mean,' sighed Zig. He lifted his head to regard the actor striding down the central aisle towards the stage. 'Hal, for the love of God, please do not skewer me during performances for the sake of a realistic death for the Beaufort Pretender. My agent will never forgive you.'

'Wouldn't dream of it, Zigmund, me old China,' laughed Hal Blackheath. He was small and slight but leapt nimbly up to join his co-stars. 'What are you up to?'

Zig, back in his faux armour, turned in an instant from a lively young actor to a wan, fearful wannabe warrior.

'Aye, must they die,' he declaimed, 'for if their father truly made them bastards, why then, Richard is truly England's king; but if their uncle lies and their birth is true, then Prince Edward will be raised to kingliness and I, despite a mother's promise, am naught but vassal and pretender.'

Chris rose to the moment as William, deepening his voice. Even his beard seemed to bristle with the mettle of a medieval warrior. 'My earl of Richmond, Lady Beaufort beheld a holy vision, her son raised high, a dragon at his shoulder, bannered all around in green and gold, with cries of triumph ringing to the heavens!'

'And so my future she proclaimed for today and all of time!'

'When time is come, I will find these downy boys,' promised Chris, as Henry Tudor's faithful standard-bearer, 'and while you proclaim their honest birth, and marry you their sweet sister to give your claim sinew, I will despatch them in a trice, and make the throne safe for thee.'

'Enough!' shouted Zig-as-Henry. 'Courage, do not desert me, for I will be king or dust, hereafter!'

Hal applauded them heartily, and Zig and Chris bowed. Vita only cocked an eyebrow at them.

'Perhaps congratulations can be saved for when you've nailed the swordfight choreography?' she suggested drily.

*

Hal and Zig moved slowly through the sequence of sword blows with their stage weapons, getting used to the weight of them in their hands. Once they had a rhythm, they rehearsed their lines as they swung, Zig as Henry Tudor taunting Hal's King Richard with Lady Beaufort's vision of her triumphant son. Then they rehearsed the death blow, Henry falling, clasping the stage blade to his side. Chris as William Brandon flung himself, weeping, to the ground at Henry's side and covered the body with the dragon-emblazoned Welsh flag before begging the magnanimous Richard for his own life.

Suitably spared, the scene ended, Chris whipped the dragon at Henry's shoulder away again to allow Zig to sit up.

'How are we doing the daisies again?' Chris asked Vita.

'The *rudbeckia*,' she said, emphasizing the flower's proper name, 'will fall out of the flag.'

'Do we have to do that?' Chris asked, trying to fold the flag up again and making a tangle. 'In the rush they'll probably just fall out all over the stage before I get to him. Shakespeare's line about "August's yellow suns" making a "graveyard bower" for Henry is enough. The audience can pretend. Suspension of disbelief and all.'

'Margaret Beaufort's vision was Henry in a field of green and gold, and that's what we're having. I'm the director and I want paper flowers, so we're having paper flowers.'

'Fine, fine, but can we get them soon? I need to practise.'

'We have plenty of time. It's two weeks till the king's Saint Day.'

'So we'll have the flowers tomorrow?'

'We will have the flowers tomorrow,' she promised.

*

Hal and Matilda Dench were rehearsing Richard and Joanna's scene at the end of the play, when the famously devout Portuguese princess arrived to marry the king. The cast, stagehands and crew were ranged about, watching the two actors wring heightened emotion from the gentle exchange.

Vikram, in his sky-blue turban today, was hand-stitching Velcro to Zig's pantaloons to match the tab glued under the back of the troublesome breastplate. 'It is really ridiculous,' he muttered to Zig, at his left, 'that some people still think King Richard ever planned to marry his niece. Hadn't he already started negotiations with Portugal for Joanna?'

'Didn't she really want to be a nun?' Zig muttered, hunched between Chris and Vikram.

'Yeah, but her brother was the king of Portugal, so that was never going to happen,' said Vikram.

'Uncle Dickon made a good alliance for an ex-princess,' said Chris over Zig's head. 'Little Elizabeth York went and married Joanna's cousin Manuel and got to be queen of Portugal. Richard even saw the bastard princes decently married. Tudor wouldn't have done that.'

Zig felt surly on his character's behalf. Henry Tudor might be ranked alongside Iago as one of Shakespeare's best villains, but he wasn't all bad.

Chris nudged Zig's shoulder. 'You were just as defensive about Macbeth when you played him.'

'The real Macbeth killed the real Duncan in battle, not in bed.'

'Shakespeare wasn't writing documentaries, Zig.'

'Oh, isn't that the truth!' grinned Vikram.

'Quiet out there!' barked Vita at them, then, to the

stage, 'Go ahead, Richard!'

'Joanna, pious and pure, I loved my Anne and Ned so well that I shall tuck you here beside them in my heart,' said Hal. He so embodied Richard's mixed feelings at this moment that his face shone with sorrow, relief and hope. 'To cherish you, as I cherished those now gone. Pray, counsel me in goodness, for which you are famed. Give me tender joy, as I shall hope to give you like. Together, let us heal this cracked and weary heart, and so too this sundered land, and let division forever be resolved.'

Matilda's role was small, but she brought a mesmerizing grace to the woman who became the mother of two Plantagenet kings and a queen of Scotland.

'Gentle Richard,' she said, with a paper garland of green and gold rudbeckia daisies in her hair, 'your good heart and my piety shall be married. I will give up my convent and make my lord my church, kneel to thee, and give thee sons and blessed daughters. My dowry be this prayer to join in yours: To heal this ruptured kingdom and bring it again to God's glory, and to yours.'

The young princes were welcomed back to the court, ushered in by their aunt Margaret of Burgundy, and Richard magnanimously gave them land and titles in exchange for their loyalty. The young Dickon cheerfully pledged his oath, but the actor portraying the former Prince Edward did a good job of his grudging acquiescence, a small hint of the next play to come in Shakespeare's Richard trilogy.

Zig leaned against Chris's shoulder. 'Imagine what England might have been like if Edward's attempt to take the throne had worked.'

Chris rested his cheek on top of Zig's head. 'Never would have happened. He'd have had to drum up more support for his claim from Tudor's old allies, but the evidence of his father's bigamy was right there on record. No, the bigger question is, what would England be like if *Richard* had died at Bosworth instead? Would we still be majority Catholic, or would the Reformation have made a bigger impact earlier? '

'Would Cromwell have still rebelled against King John?' Zig wondered.

'Would our King Richard VII be some other king celebrating some other Name Day?'

'St Charles the Reformer!' crowed Zig.

'Would Shakespeare have written more historically accurate plays?' challenged Vikram.

'Would Shakespeare have even existed?' asked Zig, and then they all went quiet.

'It would be a tragedy if he didn't,' said Zig.

'We wouldn't have met without Shakespeare,' agreed Chris. He kissed the top of Zig's head. 'So let's thank God for Richard, England and St George!'

Author's Note
I fell in love with Shakespeare's plays at a young age and despite the egregious historical inaccuracies, his Tragedy of Richard III *is one of my favourites for its dark wit, complex motivations and the nature of his fictional Richard. I've long wanted to find a way to write an alternative Shakespearean play and finally I had my chance! The title comes from* Macbeth, *and its reference to Macbeth being addressed by a title which he thinks doesn't belong to him. In history, Henry Tudor is the one in borrowed robes – here is my take on an alternative version of that history.*

About the author

Narrelle M. Harris (she/her) writes across genres, her works including paranormal adventures, crime fiction, het and queer romance, Holmes/Watson mysteries, songs and poetry. Recent fiction includes *The She Wolf of Baker Street* (2024), and her vampire novel, *The Opposite of Life*, has recently been optioned for a film. Narrelle's collection, *Scar Tissue and Other Stories*, was shortlisted in the 2019 Aurealis Awards. She has also edited four anthologies, including *The Only One in the*

World: A Sherlock Holmes Anthology (2021) and *Clamour and Mischief* (2022), which was nominated for an Aurealis award.

Website: https://narrellemharris.iwriter.com.au/

The Banbury Road

Nancy Northcott

Warwick, 2nd April 1471

Will George keep his word?
The question had gnawed at George's younger brother, Richard, duke of Gloucester all day. Now his other brother, King Edward IV, had summoned him to his chamber.

With a silver goblet in one hand, Edward lounged in one of two x-shaped chairs flanking a square table. On the table sat a silver pitcher, another goblet, and a small, silver plate of red and white gingerbread squares arranged in a chequerboard pattern.

Early evening light from the mullioned window above it revealed lines of strain in Edward's face. No wonder. Whether or not George, who happened to be duke of Clarence by the king's grace, kept his word and brought the soldiers he'd promised to tomorrow's rendezvous would make a great difference in Edward's campaign to regain his throne.

Edward gestured with his goblet towards the other chair. 'Pray, sit, Dickon. Have some wine, and let us be comfortable.'

His use of Richard's nickname signalled that this was to be a talk between brothers, not between a king and his liege man. Plain speaking, then, would be his expectation. So much the better, especially if they were to discuss their wayward brother.

Richard sat and poured himself wine. He glanced around the panelled chamber with its large bed curtained in fine green wool, ornate clothing chest, and rush matting on the floor. A tapestry of a hunt scene hung above the chest.

'I must say, sire, the mayor offers us better housing than our camp tents.'

'He's grateful we merely wish to occupy the town, not embroil it in a siege against the castle.'

Edward had seen no point in trying to take the castle. His forces were safe in the town for now, and staying anywhere for long, as a siege would require, wouldn't help him regain his throne. The castle's defenders need not worry unless they foolishly provoked the king.

'I imagine he is,' Richard said. Regardless, Edward's welcome here would last only until the rebel earl of Warwick appeared on the horizon with an army. Because he was currently behind the walls of Coventry, having thrice refused Edward's challenge to do battle, he wouldn't pose a problem tonight.

Edward's gaze became distracted. He frowned.

Rather than break the silence, Richard sipped the rich, red Flemish wine. Edward would reveal the reason for his summons when he was ready.

From the street outside came the sounds of noblemen hailing their servants and of servants calling to each other. Under it all, more distant, lay the rumble of the soldiers' voices in conversation. A rough baritone launched into a raucous song about a tavern maid named Biddable Bess. Other voices joined in.

Richard barely noticed the song, a lewd but amusing one delivered with enthusiasm. These men were prepared to lay down their lives to support Edward in regaining his throne. The men George had agreed to bring would greatly increase their chances of success. Unless George and his allies in rebellion, Warwick and the deposed King Henry VI's queen, Margaret of Anjou, had been playing Edward and his lords for fools all along.

With a direct look, Edward said, 'Father and Edmund died because men who pledged their loyalty, who came to Sandal Castle vowing to fight under Father's banner and in his cause, turned on him in battle.'

Richard had known that, but he hadn't related the incident to their present situation. George, after all, was family. Even though he hadn't behaved as such.

'If you're concerned that George may not keep his word, I can only guess that he will. If he is wise at all, I think he must.' Though wisdom had rarely been George's governing trait. Richard continued, 'He now has less chance of succeeding to the throne than he ever did, so the most he can hope for out of this rebellion is some additional land. He'll fare better at your side than at a Lancastrian court where he's likely despised. I cannot see any other path that would offer him as great a benefit, let alone a greater one.'

'Which, of course, is George's primary concern.' Edward shook his head.

'Alas, I fear it is. He wasn't always thus, you know. When *Maman* sent us to Burgundy after Father was killed, George looked out for me. He assured me all would be well.' At age ten, George had been only three years older than Richard but much more confident, enviably so. 'He had a way of winning the Burgundians around us to our side, at least outwardly, so they were not merely courteous but friendly. You have that same skill.' With a grimace, Richard added, 'Would that I did.'

'You win men in your own way. Your dealings in Wales and the West Country prove that.'

Richard blinked in surprise.

Gesturing towards the window, Edward said, 'I see who came at your call, brother. William Herbert and the Harringtons are the most notable, but there are others. Once you win men, they trust you. Perhaps because they know you'll not turn your coat on them.'

'Thank you, sire – ah, Ned,' Richard managed, hastily amending his reply at a look from Edward.

Edward rose to pace. When Richard also would have risen, as etiquette required, his brother waved him back to his seat, asking, 'When do you think George became so ... acquisitive?'

Acquisitive. A better word than greedy but meaning much the same.

'I cannot say. When we returned to England from Burgundy and he realized he was your heir, he seemed much impressed with the honours you bestowed on him.' Richard paused, weighing his words. ''Tis fair to say he was a bit inclined to crow about it. I think perhaps the news of your marriage to Queen Elizabeth, the implication that you would soon have heirs of your body, may have shaken him.'

Edward raised an eyebrow. 'He cannot truly have expected otherwise.'

'I don't know what was in his mind. We were together less often after we returned. Once I went into Warwick's household, George and I rarely met.' That time under Warwick's tutelage had meant much to him, which made the earl's treason that much more painful. 'He and I are royal dukes because of you. We have titles and extensive lands. I'm grateful. He also should be, and he must know that. Perhaps he is grateful, whether or not he admits it.'

'If so, his gratitude is sparse.' Edward dropped into his chair again. Frowning, he toyed with a red square of gingerbread but didn't take it. 'I forgave him for marrying Isabel Neville against my will. He repaid me by joining Warwick's efforts to make me their puppet king. I assumed the nobility's refusal to come to a Parliament ordered by Warwick – their lack of support for that scheme generally – would have shown both George and Warwick the folly of trying to supplant me. Again, I forgave them. And how did they thank me? By trying, less than a year later, to depose me and put George in my place.'

Richard knew all this, of course, but Edward seemed to need to share his frustration. He banged his fist on his knee.

'I was far too lenient. But now, needing the men George is to bring me, and with *Maman* and our sisters urging me to forgive him, I must stay my hand yet again.'

He took a long swallow of his wine and frowned.

Into the brooding silence, Richard said, 'You've faced many difficult choices, Ned.' Not least overlooking George's defiant marriage to Warwick's daughter, giving that lord a link to the throne that Edward had opposed. 'We're fortunate that most of the lords also refused to support this second rebellion.'

The failure of the puppet king scheme nearly a year and a half ago might have persuaded Warwick and – repugnant as Richard found the thought – George that their best course this time was to kill Edward as soon as they could. If they'd managed to capture him, they well might have done so. No one had ever said as much, but Richard had no doubt they had considered it.

'The lords refused,' Edward ground out, 'until Warwick thought to put old King Henry back on the throne. Espousing his cause and allying with his queen and heir has bought Warwick enough support to be dangerous.' Bitterness laced the words. Edward again rose to pace, waving at Richard to stay seated.

Richard couldn't blame him for his anger. Edward had narrowly escaped capture the previous autumn and had fled to Burgundy with Richard and a few others. Their sister Margaret, Burgundy's duchess, had prevailed upon her husband to offer them shelter.

Richard said, 'We should be grateful Henry's queen insisted that her son, not George, be his father's heir.' As she had done when Richard and Edward's father had been part of a settlement supplanting the Lancastrian prince a dozen years earlier. The queen's resolve had led to their father's death.

Edward scowled at his wine. 'Aye, because only thwarted ambition could bring George home.'

That and the efforts of their mother and sisters to bring about a rapprochement. At least George's defection from the rebels would bring additional troops to Edward's banner. If he kept his word.

A fortnight ago, with support from Burgundy, Edward had led his companions back to England to reclaim his throne. Now, though, they balanced on a knife's edge while they waited to see whether George would deliver the men he promised and return to the Yorkist cause, or whether the hope he might was in truth the bait for an elaborate trap.

'I appreciate your loyalty, Dickon.' Edward sat again, running a hand through his hair. 'Your Burgundian exile after Father died brought you and George close, at least for a while. That may be why he and *Maman* agreed you should be his direct conduit to me these past weeks. Shared exile did much the same for you and me last year. Our time in Bruges confirmed my impression of you from your actions, so the men who've come to your side don't surprise me.'

Over Richard's thanks, Edward continued, 'I must ask you to trust that I'll not forget your loyalty. That I'll reward you for it in due time.'

Frowning, Richard replied, 'I but did my duty as your subject and your brother.' Any man would welcome lands and offices that would increase his wealth, but he'd acted from honour, not from expectation of riches.

'I know you did.' Edward emphasized his answer with a nod. '*Maman* made plain the need to reward George for doing what he should've done from the start. His most recent letter to you, of course, reinforced that.'

'George could not do otherwise.' A wiser man might refrain, but George showed no forethought in his dealings with this brother.

'Of course not,' Edward repeated in a dry voice. 'Pardoning George means I'll not have his lands to reward those of greater loyalty.'

'And the same if you pardon Warwick.' The rebel earl's extensive holdings, some by right of his wife, would have served as lavish rewards.

'Aye, but, between us, I hope he'll refuse the pardon.'

'Why?' Richard had quietly hoped the earl would see reason and beg for the king's forgiveness. Both Richard and Edward owed him much from the days when he'd been a loyal supporter of the Yorkist cause.

'Because I'll have no more overmighty subjects. He could not have created the mischief he has if he were a lesser landholder.'

The reference to *overmighty subjects* struck a chord in Richard, who blinked.

'What?' Edward demanded.

'King Henry and Queen Margaret might've said the same of Father.'

'They might well. Unlike Warwick, though, he would've kept faith with them had they not forced his hand. I would not like to order the earl's death, but I'll do what I must.'

No matter how much any of them regretted it.

Richard stared at the wall tapestry without truly seeing it. He'd been seven when their father and brother had been slain.

'I wish I could have spent more time with Father. And with Edmund. I've only the haziest memories.'

'I wish we all could have. They would be deeply proud of you. As *Maman* is.'

She'd never told Richard that. Warmed by his brother's words, he replied, 'I hope so.'

'Trust me on that, little brother. 'Tis not because she likes George best that she lavishes so much attention on him.' Edward waited until Richard looked back at him to add, ''Tis because he's the one she most worries about letting his conceit lead him into trouble.'

'As it has done this time.'

'Aye, it has. He's fortunate that we need the men coming with him to add to our ranks. If we didn't, *Maman*'s wish or not, I would not be so generous.'

By the same token, if this was a trick – if those

men attacked the royal forces instead of joining them – the king and his lords faced a hard battle.

Richard glanced at the gingerbread, but this discussion left him with no appetite for the sweet.

'How much latitude do you mean to give George in future?'

'Not much.' Edward grimaced. 'As long as *Maman* lives, I'll do my best to keep him content, but he had best tread carefully.'

If only they could assume George would understand that.

Edward directed a keen look at Richard. 'When we meet George, if aught seems amiss to you, I rely on you to speak up at once.'

Richard met his brother's gaze squarely. 'I'll always guard your back.'

'I've come to take that for granted.' Edward flashed the smile that so readily won him friends, but with the extra warmth he reserved for family. Before Richard could reply, he added, 'Now we both should make our preparations for the morrow.'

Richard bade his brother a good night. As he walked down the rush mattings in the corridor to his own chamber, he had only one thought in mind: *Please let me be right about George.*

*

The king's army left Warwick, marching south towards Banbury, as the church bells rang *terce*, the midmorning canonical hour. The tramp of marching feet, the clip-clops of hooves, the jingle of harness, and the flapping of banners in the breeze had become familiar these past weeks. So had the way the sunlight shining through the silk brightened the colours.

Richard rode at Edward's right hand. On the king's other side, William, Lord Hastings and Anthony Woodville, Lord Rivers, who'd been their companions in exile, kept pace with them. Hastings was a stocky man with a square-jawed face, thick brown hair and an amiable demeanour. He'd been fiercely loyal to Edward, and that mattered more now than his tendency to encourage the king in dissolute revels.

Rivers, Edward's brother by marriage, was taller, with a thin face and a contemplative air that easily gave way to a smile. His family owed Edward much, and Rivers was not one to forget that. Where Hastings was quick to react, Rivers weighed his choices. Richard liked that about the earl.

Because the scouts assured the king no hostile force lurked near, the army travelled without armour. Scouts in Edward's livery, murrey and blue tunics with a sun in splendour on the left breast, rode back and forth between their forces and George's so each would know of the other's approach. They confirmed that George's force also travelled without armour, a good sign.

They passed by fields lined by dry-stone walls and hedgerows, and through a wood with oak trees shading the road. Mounted, Richard sat high enough to see over the hedges to winter barley that must be almost ready for harvest.

The two armies stopped about half a mile apart between fields bordered by hedgerows.

As agreed, George rode forward with two other men clad in fine wool and linen. Behind him, a rider bore his standard, the black bull of Clarence.

Edward rode to meet him. Richard, Rivers and Hastings accompanied him, keeping their relative positions but remaining half a length behind. Behind them came Edward's mounted standard bearer and a trio of squires on foot to manage the horses when the men dismounted.

The two groups met halfway between the armies.

Also as agreed, George and his companions dismounted and knelt in the road. On George's brown hair sat a velvet cap pinned with a sapphire surrounded by pearls. Below it, his square face showed no expression, a sign that he concealed some strong feeling. The shadows below his eyes, though, and the faint lines bracketing his mouth betrayed unease leading to this moment.

Was that unease dread of Edward's reaction? Or tension because of planned treachery? Or dislike of humbling himself? *Please let it be only his dislike of asking for pardon.*

Twenty paces away, Edward and his companions also dismounted. The group followed the king as he strode forwards.

George squared his shoulders. 'I have erred grievously and offended Your Grace by my foolish alliance with Your Grace's enemies. I most humbly beseech Your Grace to pardon me for my folly. In token of my loyalty and in hopes of atoning for my error, I bring five thousand men to aid Your Grace in regaining the throne.'

Edward said naught for a long moment. Richard's neck tensed.

Then the king smiled, the effect like sunlight breaking through lowering clouds. He reached down to help George rise.

'I do gladly pardon you, brother.' As they embraced, he added, 'Welcome. Truly, George, 'tis good to see you again.'

'I thank you, Ned. I am also glad to see you.' As the king released him, George's gaze met Richard's. 'Dickon, well met.'

They also embraced.

Edward turned to Anthony Woodville on his left. 'Lord Rivers, see to the joining of the duke's force with ours.'

'Gladly, sire.'

George nodded to one of the men with him, a stocky, middle-aged man in a green wool tunic and darker green cap. Richard didn't recognize the livery badge on the cap's upturned brim. Rivers led the man to the far side of the road.

'If I may, sire,' George said, 'I would speak privily with our brother, Gloucester.'

'If he wishes it,' Edward replied, cocking an eyebrow at Richard.

With a slight bow, Richard said, 'Of course.'

He and George walked together to the near side of the road, out of earshot if they kept their voices low. The king and Lord Hastings stood talking with George's other companions.

George stopped with his back to the road.

'I'm grateful for your help, Dickon.'

That was surprising. George generally assumed his family owed him whatever he wanted and saved his gratitude for those rare men he believed owed him naught.

'Repairing the breach gladdens me, George. If that's all—'

'Will he keep his word? Edward?'

'He asked me the same question yesterday about you.' George's doubts made sense. Although he would never admit it, even he must know he richly deserved to be scorned.

Resentment flashed through George's blue eyes. 'I have little choice, given Warwick's alliance with that witch Henry made his queen. I've turned over my army now, and I'm in Ned's power, no matter how much we choose to hang ribbons on that truth.'

'He will keep his word.' Richard replied, his tone even. As expected, George didn't realize how little he deserved the grace Edward was showing him. 'He has promised *Maman* as well, you know.'

'A lovely sentiment, but she has no more power to compel him than you do. I'm risking all on your assurances, little brother.'

That term from Edward had held affection. From George, it carried condescension that grated.

Richard took a slow breath. He should lead George back to the others. Should insist on it. But that remark was beyond enough.

'George, you're a royal duke. You have extensive lands and wealth. Why is that not enough for you?'

George scowled, the anger in his face so sharp that Richard almost took a step back.

'It should all be mine,' he hissed. 'All of it. I'm Father's true heir, not Ned.'

Shock held Richard motionless. His amazement must have registered with his brother. George's anger faded, and he looked down at his feet, though he still had a stubborn set to his jaw.

Why would he—? Oh, surely not! But what else could be his reason?

'You cannot believe that absurd tale about *Maman* and the Rouen archer? Margaret told me about that. 'Tis but French gossip meant to discomfit Ned.'

'You cannot know that,' George muttered.

'As duchess of Burgundy, Margaret surely knows the ploys of her French enemy. Is this what Warwick told you? Is this how he persuaded you to join in his treason?'

'Gently,' George snapped. 'I'm welcomed back to my family, remember?'

'Not if you spout such as that, you're not. That, too, is treason.'

From the corner of his eye, Richard saw Ned watching them. He forced his lips into a smile.

'If *Maman* heard you say that, she would have you strung up by your bollocks, royal duke or not.' George opened his mouth, but Richard overrode him. 'For all our sakes, I'll forget you espoused this absurd claim. Unless, that is, I hear of you saying it anywhere ever again. If I do, I'll have no choice but to bring it to the king's attention.'

George's eyes widened in surprise, perhaps because Richard had never spoken thus to him. Well, perhaps it was time he realized his *little brother* had grown up.

'Do you understand me?' Richard demanded, still smiling.

George studied him for a moment. At last, he

softly replied, 'So the puppy has teeth. Yes, *Gloucester*, I understand you.'

Richard nodded. 'Very well.'

Behind George, Rivers directed the intermingling of the two forces. Men shuffled along the road, realigning themselves so the king's men would lead the march northward and both armies' baggage trains would travel at the rear.

'If that's all,' Richard said, 'allow me to say I grieve the loss of your babe. I hope Isabel is well.'

'Thank you, Dickon. It was ... difficult for us all.' Weariness showed plainly in George's face now. 'My lady was well enough when last I saw her. I pray she remains so.'

With her father, Warwick, in rebellion and her husband now set against him, Isabel must have myriad worries. Her sister, Anne, had been wed to the Lancastrian heir despite lifelong loyalty to York. She, too, must have worries. Richard pitied them, but he could do naught to help them. His loyalty belonged to Edward.

He nodded and clapped George on the shoulder.

'Let us carry on with the day. Now that you're with us, we march to Coventry to confront Warwick.'

'I'll do my best to bring him to terms, as I promised.'

'I hope you can.' However unlikely that seemed.

They walked back to the others, most of whom were clustered further down the road as the armies realigned. Edward stood alone, watching the soldiers move. George halted by Hastings, a short distance from the king. Richard took what he was coming to think of as his place, at Edward's right hand.

'Problem?' the king murmured. 'You were scowling.'

Richard answered softly, 'George thought my appreciation of his arrival insufficient.'

If George had even half his wits, he would take Richard's warning to heart. If a time came when the king had to confront that outlandish claim, matters would not go well for the duke of Clarence.

'So we are back to our old patterns, then.'

'It appears so, sire.'

'I had hoped for better.' Edward shook his head. 'See if you can assist Anthony in combining these forces. The sooner we reach Coventry and deal with Warwick, the better.'

*

The next evening, Richard waited in the king's pavilion outside Coventry. Edward sat in silence in the large chair that served as a throne. Richard perched on a stool by the trestle table, while Hastings, Rivers and others lounged on chairs or stools. George had gone under a flag of truce to negotiate with Warwick. Until Edward knew the outcome of those talks, he wouldn't decide their next move.

Pages brought ale and gingerbread, but no one had much appetite.

Edward sat still, as though carved from stone. Did he never betray tension or unease in public? Richard would've given much for such poise.

Hastings rubbed the back of his neck. Rivers ran a rosary idly through his fingers.

The tent's entry flap was flung open and George stepped inside. Judging by the grim set of his mouth, his mission had not succeeded.

He bowed to Edward. 'Your Grace.'

'My lord duke. What news?'

'Alas, sire, but Lord Warwick refuses Your Grace's kind offer. He declares he'll receive no further emissaries.'

Edward's eyes glinted, but he spoke in a calm, level voice.

'So be it, then. Be seated, Clarence. How did Warwick seem to you? Describe his manner.'

A page entered with a mug of something.

Accepting it, George sighed.

'He's vexed with me, as we expected, but he seems confident. I believe he expects Queen Margaret and Edward of Lancaster to land any day. They'll bring men at arms with them, of course, and Warwick has always thought men would flock to their banner who'll not come to his.'

'What do you think?' Edward asked.

'Henry's queen is resolved to have the crown for her son at any cost.' George paused to take a sip of his drink. ''Tis no overstatement to say she despises us all to the core of her soul. Especially you, Your Grace. She will not give way, and there may well be men who've not answered Warwick's call but will fight under her banner.'

Edward rubbed his chin. 'After speaking with him, how many such do you think there are?'

'He said naught of that, so I hold with our earlier estimate of perhaps a dozen, more or less. Most of the major lords have chosen sides or decided not to, though some may be waiting to see how matters develop.'

'Then we must ensure they develop in our favour.' Edward swirled his mug, looking down into it. 'As we discussed last night, I'll not risk becoming entangled in a siege here while Margaret marches towards us with fresh troops. No, my lords, we're for London. We'll find support there and on the road south.'

And Edward would finally see his queen and his children again, including, for the first time, his son and heir, Edward. The boy had been born in sanctuary at Westminster in November, during his father's exile.

'We break camp in the morning,' the king said, 'and march south as soon as we may. Let Warwick huddle behind Coventry's walls and hope for salvation from France. While he does, we'll build our forces to be ready for a decisive battle. We cannot stop Margaret from landing, nor should we. 'Tis best we defeat her and her son beyond all recovery. England will never have peace until we shatter the Lancastrian claim.'

He glanced around at them all.

'We've much to do this evening. When you've given the necessary orders, return here. We'll dine well and retire early. Tomorrow, we take the next step in reclaiming our realm.'

Richard walked out with George. As the other men hurried away, George put a hand on his brother's arm.

'About what I said on the road.'

'I don't understand.' Richard raised his brows.

'You know what I mean. I shouldn't have said that. Yes, Warwick convinced me the old story about *Maman* and an archer in Rouen was true. I shouldn't have listened.'

'What changed your mind?' Assuming it had changed, that this was not some ruse on George's part to allay Richard's suspicions.

'Warwick's manner today. He was so righteous, so inflamed with his own cause. Yes, he helped Ned to the throne, but that gave him no cause to consider himself the power behind that throne. He did, you know. I shouldn't have listened to him, nor said aught about it. I feared Ned would betray me despite his pledges and yours.' George shrugged. 'He has made me welcome, as he promised, and I regret my distrust.'

'I understand,' Richard replied. Yet George was unlikely to give up a story that could – in the right circumstances – benefit him later. He was entirely capable of dissembling. But challenging him would only cause strife. Regaining Edward's throne required united action. Best to dissemble, himself, and keep an eye on George.

Smiling, he clapped George on the shoulder. 'I'm glad to hear that. We are the three sons of York. Together we are a powerful force.'

'Indeed.' Apparently satisfied, George bade Richard farewell and strode towards his own pavilion.

Richard watched him go. Please God, naught would ever lead George to think he should trot out that tale. Edward had said George must *tread carefully*, and he'd meant it. One could never rely upon George to do that, but perhaps circumstances – and the royal rewards coming his way – would satisfy him.

But that was a problem for the future, perhaps a future that would never arrive. In the near term, they had a kingdom to win.

About the author

Nancy Northcott is the author of the Ricardian-themed historical fantasy trilogy *The Boar King's Honor*. She currently has seventeen books available, a mixture of historical fantasy, science fiction, and several types of romance. They have been published by Grand Central/Hachette, Falstaff Books and independently. Her debut novel, *Renegade* (now titled *Renegade Mage*), received a starred review from *Library Journal*, which called it 'genre fiction at its best'.

A history nerd since grade school, Nancy has an undergraduate degree in history and a law degree. Reading *The Daughter of Time*, at the urging of a law school classmate, spurred her to become a Ricardian. She has taught cultural studies courses at university level and has given presentations on Richard III and the Wars of the Roses to university classes studying Shakespeare's *Richard III.*

Nancy would like everyone to remember that Shakespeare made things up for a living.

Website:	https://www.NancyNorthcott.com
Books:	https://www.amazon.com/stores/Nancy-Northcott/author/B00ITY5KLS
Free sample:	https://dl.bookfunnel.com/2dboypbzh5 (*The Boar King's Honor*)

There Will Be a Wedding

Brian Wainwright

Middleham Castle, 1475–6

When Thomas, Lord Scrope of Masham died in the autumn of 1475 – not many months after King Edward returned from his abortive invasion of France – he was a much-mourned man. As landlords and masters went, the judgement of the alehouses of Masham was that he had been a good one.

Over their ale – Masham ale, the best in all Yorkshire – men pondered as to what the future might hold. The heir, also Thomas, was the eldest of four sons, but still a stripling. He would not come into his own until aged twenty-one, five years and more into the future. All knew that he would go into wardship, and a rapacious guardian could do a lot of damage in five years. A guardian might revise rents, chase up arrears with more ferocity than the late Lord Scrope had ever thought to do. He might concern himself about the fate of the odd coney, or enquire into use made of the lord's waste lands by some people who pastured their sheep on them without such formalities as rent. He might even go so far as to query why pigs rooted in the lord's woods, in certain places where no right of pannage existed. All manner of awkward questions might be asked, especially if the guardian proved to be a 'foreigner'. By this they meant anyone from outside the North Riding of Yorkshire.

The family at Masham Castle was just as concerned for their future as were their tenants, though they scarcely spoke of it. After the funeral, when they were busy with all the formalities and prayers and the hospitality for dozens of guests, and after the Month Mind, they relapsed into a thoughtful silence.

Elizabeth, Lady Scrope was not a woman who valued her own independence. She could manage a household as efficiently as anyone; she never ordered too little salted fish for Lent or too much wine for Christmas. Her people's liveries never grew shabby before they were replaced, and her children were all clean, courteous and well-presented, as befitted the sons and daughters of a lord. She rarely wasted a penny, and was not afraid to mend clothing with her own stitches or to make up shirts and shifts with her own hands.

However, the thought of managing her dower properties, of having dealings with bailiffs and land agents, or pursuing legal quarrels with neighbours, quite daunted her. She resolved, therefore, to marry again. There had already been several offers, for, although she would never see eighteen again, she was both a handsome and a capable woman – an excellent prospect for a man with judgement and maturity enough to value her.

Her choice fell upon Gilbert Talbot, younger son of the second earl of Shrewsbury. That Shrewsbury had been hacked to death at Northampton, fighting for Lancaster, but Gilbert had made his peace with King Edward, and served at court as carver and king's esquire. He had lands in Shropshire and in Ireland, and was a handsome, well-mannered fellow in his middle twenties. Nonetheless, the alehouses of Masham were bewildered, for he was not a Yorkshireman. The decision was decried as a woman's folly, though a minority argued it spoke well for Lady Scrope that she could attract an admirer almost young enough to be her son.

Lady Scrope now rode through the snow to Middleham Castle to settle matters with the duke of Gloucester. She had had preliminary discussions with him when she attended the Christmas festivities there with her children, but there was bargaining to be done and the arrangements to be set down in ink by clerks, perused by lawyers and sealed with the seals of the principals.

Some, even in Yorkshire, found Richard of Gloucester intimidating. Idle clerks, corrupt officials and oppressive landlords had some cause to, for the least *they* could expect was to be seared by his coruscating wit. (Some would have preferred to be flogged rather than endure it.) Lady Scrope was none of these things, and she knew that a man so kind to his women and his dogs was by no means to be feared. Their negotiations ran smoothly. At no point did Richard cry 'Loved be God!', which was another man's 'You cannot be serious!'

The duke was a similar age to her prospective husband, Gilbert Talbot. Not so handsome, Lady Scrope thought, but certainly as courteous. Not as heavily built as Gilbert either, but not lacking in strength or courage. He was a proven warrior, veteran of the bloodbaths of Barnet and Tewkesbury, as well as of sundry skirmishes with their troublesome neighbours across the Scottish border. His voice was a little deeper than one might expect from a man with so light a frame, but it was also gentle, persuasive, almost lyrical.

He drove a hard bargain – all Yorkshire would have mocked him had he been unduly liberal – but not an unjust one, given their relative places in the world. Her son Thomas was to enter into his service and be 'ruled and guided' by him in all things. In return, all that was Scrope of Masham was taken into the friendly fortress of his protection, against any whatsoever. There was more to it than this, of course. Lawyers' quibbles. But that was the nub of the indenture they both signed and sealed and which they divided between them so each had a copy.

So the young Lord Scrope became a member of Gloucester's household, and rode to Middleham with two men to attend him, since even a young baron in wardship must have some retinue to ride at his back and this was as modest a following as was thought decent. Thomas was not unhappy with the arrangement. All spoke well of Richard of Gloucester as master and patron. Besides, he was growing weary of living at home with brothers he thought of as babies and sisters he scarcely thought of at all.

Almost before he knew it, he was clad in Gloucester's livery and kneeling at the duke's feet to kiss his hand in token of fealty. Richard did not keep him kneeling long. Instead, he seated him at his side in a window embrasure that looked out over the courtyard.

Thomas held his tongue, knowing well enough that it was not for him to initiate conversation. They appraised each other in silence for a moment, the duke's grey eyes running over the youth as though measuring him for new clothes. A faint smile implied that he liked what he saw.

'Welcome to Middleham,' he said.

'I thank Your Grace.'

'Wine?'

'If it pleases you, Your Grace.'

Again the smile. 'If it did not, I should not have offered it.' He leaned to reach a jug on the adjoining dresser, carefully poured two glasses of the rich red liquid. One he handed to Thomas. 'By the way, you need not keep calling me "Your Grace" at every answer. Not when we are in private. "Cousin" is quite sufficient. I dare swear we are cousins of some degree; if not, we may think ourselves as such by courtesy.'

'Thank you, Your Grace.'

'Cousin. There is a time and a season for full formality. You will have chance enough to serve me on bended knee, to stand before me with your head bared and all the rest of it. Not every hour of the day, Thomas. I may be your guardian and your lord, but I hope we shall be friends. I also trust that you will be happy in my household until it's time for you to possess your own.'

There was silence for a moment. Each took a taste of his wine, watching the other over his glass.

'I take it you have already been trained in arms?' Richard asked.

'Yes, Your – I mean, Cousin. My father saw to that. I started with wooden swords when I was but eight, and worked on from there.'

'I expected as much. I know Warwick valued your father very highly and Warwick's judgement – in most matters – was sound. He knew a worthy man when he saw one. Warwick trained me, Thomas, as you may know. I loved him, sorrowed that ever he turned against the king. I see myself as his heir. Not only as his daughter's husband and lord of half his lands. Do you take my meaning?'

Thomas was not sure that he did. 'I think so, Cousin.'

'Men would have followed Warwick to the gates of hell. My ambition is to earn such loyalty. *Earn* it, you understand. Only a fool demands it as of right.'

*

It did not take long for Thomas Scrope to settle into Gloucester's household, for he was not given to boast or lightly to quarrel and he was apt to take his fellows at their own estimation. He was a little too old to require much formal training, though, of course, he took part in martial exercises with his fellows – combat at the barriers, sword play and the occasional informal joust in the tiltyard. All these activities were the subject for wagers and a degree of banter, but he neither staked too high to worry about the outcome nor too low to appear mean or uncertain of his worth.

There were other duties too. Attending on Gloucester, taking turns to help him dress or undress, sometimes waiting at table, sometimes following at the duke's back when he rode out on some business or other, or went hawking or hunting, or simply decided that he was in want of air and an hour in the saddle by way of exercise.

Thomas had a fine, clerkly hand, better than that of most young nobles in these parts, some of whom could barely write at all. So it was not long before he was set to assist Robert Brackenbury, who had lately been appointed treasurer to the duke. The work consisted of taking cash from the duke's receivers and debtors, paying out for the numerous expenses of Gloucester and his household, and, of course, keeping meticulous records of both incomings and outgoings.

It was not long before Brackenbury was giving a favourable report on his pupil to the duke. 'A diligent boy,' Brackenbury said, 'and neither a fool nor an idler. He takes pride in his work and spots an error more quickly than I do myself.'

'A paragon!' cried Gloucester, with an amiable smile. 'I'm almost suspicious. Do you really find no fault in the fellow?'

Brackenbury considered for a moment. 'He has a tendency to sing over his work when he is happy.'

'A grave sin indeed!' The smile appeared again. 'Well, something must be done about it. We must find him a wife.'

*

'I'm not sure,' said the girl – and she *was* a girl, barely twelve years old – as she clutched her little dog on her lap, 'that I *want* to be married.'

'Few of us are,' said Lady Beauchamp, 'but then, my dear, you must weigh the alternatives.'

Elizabeth Neville – commonly known as Bess – stared at her through wide, brown eyes. It was said that Lady Beauchamp was the best listener in the household, and possibly the wisest member of it, but Bess did not find this response helpful. Of course, Lady Beauchamp was *old*. Even older than the duke and duchess. Not *that* far off thirty. Perhaps it was not reasonable to expect understanding from someone whose hair – hidden beneath her tall hennin – was quite possibly starting to turn grey. As for the duchess – one could not possibly speak to so august person on such a matter. The very thought made

Bess blush. And as for Lady Warwick, the duchess's mother – why, she was so old she was practically an *ancestor*, though strictly she was also Bess's aunt. She must be fifty at the least, Bess estimated.

'Perhaps you would prefer to be a nun?' Lady Beauchamp ventured. 'If you do, I know the duke will not stand in your way.'

The look of horror on the girl's face was answer enough.

'Well, convents can be very strict. I know, I lived in one for a time and it was not to my taste. Some do not even allow dogs. Imagine that!'

Bess clutched her little spaniel even more tightly, so that it let out a squeal, attracting the attention of two greyhounds that came loping across the room to check if it was a rabbit or some other legitimate prey.

'No, Garlik! No, Stalker!' said Lady Beauchamp with a firmness that couched the two animals in a moment. 'You need a livelihood, child. Some means of living. I presume you do not intend to wipe down alehouse tables or become a laundress?'

'Of course not, my lady!'

'Your parents, God assoil them, are not in this world, so cannot secure your future. Too late for them to gift you a manor or two. Would you serve in some other woman's household for the rest of your life?'

'No, my lady.'

'Then you must marry.'

'It isn't fair!'

'My dear, life isn't fair, and never has been, but it is as God wills. Look, this boy is, I judge, well enough. Nobly born, with rich lands. All speak well of him, though I dare say he has his faults like the rest of us. For all that, the duke and duchess are not monsters. If you really cannot stomach the fellow, they'll not force you. Never in this world. But consider – you cannot go on picking and choosing forever, and the next one offered to you may well be worse. There are only so many suitable men available.'

She paused, allowing the girl to consider.

'He might be as old as me, with no teeth,' she went on.

Bess gaped at the thought, although Lady Beauchamp's teeth were as near to perfect as made no difference.

'A boy that age can be moulded, as an older man cannot.'

'But …'

'Yes?'

'I'm afraid.'

Lady Beauchamp sighed. 'Bess, as my mother used to say in the matter of spiders, he is far more afraid of you than you are of him.'

'Why should he be afraid? Of *me*?'

'He's sixteen, child, and will have as much idea of what to do with a wife as he has of flying with the crows. I suggest you give him a chance. Talk to him.'

'*Talk?*'

'Yes. Talk. You may find that you like him. And if you do not, remember what I said. You have only to petition the duchess. She will never allow you to be forced.'

*

'Well?' asked the duchess, looking up from her sewing.

'She has agreed to parley,' said Lady Beauchamp, curtseying and then settling down at her cousin's side.

'*Agreed to parley?*' the countess of Warwick repeated. 'I don't know what girls are coming to these days. She should be on her knees in the chapel, thanking the Blessed Virgin that a good husband has been found for her.'

'She is a child, madam,' Lady Beauchamp replied mildly.

'Well, naturally, *you* would side with her. You always were a rebel against authority. She is twelve, which makes her a woman in the eyes of God, and, as I said, she ought to be *grateful*.'

'Mother,' said the duchess, with something of a sigh, 'this is not helpful.'

'I was *nine* when I married your father,' her mother said. 'No one asked my opinion, and I would not have dared to protest. I knew that I should be countess of Salisbury one day and that my parents had made a fine marriage for me. That sufficed.'

Lady Beauchamp struggled to think of a response that would not be disrespectful to her social superior, but could not find one. So she subsided and glanced at Duchess Anne, with a nod to serve as a prompt.

'I'm sure the child will see sense, given time,' said Anne. 'Besides, there is no haste. They'll not be bedded for a good four years yet, and that's long enough for her to change her mind half a dozen times. Let us be patient.'

'Shall I speak to the boy?' asked Lady Beauchamp.

The duchess considered that suggestion for a moment, her expression coming as close to a frown as it ever did.

'No,' she said. 'I think that is a task for Richard. I shall ask him to manage the matter.'

*

The duke of Gloucester, in his capacity as principal officer in the north of England for his brother the king, had plenty of business to occupy him, so found no difficulty in postponing this additional duty laid on him by his wife. It was, he told himself, not a matter of pressing urgency. Besides, such a conversation required the right moment. The right moment might be Michaelmas, he thought, considering the matter. Or perhaps Christmas. Or the following Easter. How did one begin?

He was glad to find an excuse to put the matter aside. One afternoon, visiting the mews to inspect his moulting falcons, he found Thomas Scrope and Bess Neville admiring Scrope's goshawk, their heads close together as the lad explained … well, something. Without a word, he shook his head to his companions and all three of them withdrew so silently that the young couple did not know they had been seen.

Sometimes, thought Richard, as he rode out of the castle with his cronies to enjoy an unplanned ride over the fells, all that a man needs to do is nothing. The matter is in the best hands, their own. Anne, after the manner of women, was worrying about nothing. He was rather satisfied by his own astute handling of the issue.

*

After some consultation – a matter of allowing the duchess and her mother to agree a timetable – Richard decided that the wedding would take place at Michaelmas, on the grounds it was as good a time as any. There was no question of a bedding, for the girl was far too young, but a canonical marriage ceremony before witnesses made the arrangement secure. The consummation would take place in due course, but that was a private matter. There need be no great ceremony for *that*.

Invitations were sent off in all directions. All Yorkshire was to come, and much of Lancashire, as well as a minority from the Palatinate of Durham. The earl of Northumberland sent his regrets, but the bride's mother and her new husband agreed to travel up from their wedded bliss in Shropshire, assuming that Sir Gilbert could be spared from his duties to King Edward. Even Lord Stanley and his lady agreed to make their way across the Pennines from the splendour of Lathom House – a surprise, this last. Richard had anticipated a polite refusal, and now was left pondering on the wisdom of sending out invitations in the expectation they would be rejected. One can be *too* courteous, he thought, making a note in the commonplace book he kept in his head.

It was not that Richard did not talk to Scrope from time to time. For one thing, Thomas was often among those in close attendance on him. There was rarely a day when they did not interact in some way. The young man was increasingly useful. He could entertain, with perfect courtesy, a visitor waiting for audience. He could be trusted to carry a letter to the lord mayor of York and bring a message back, or to ride to Barnard Castle or Sheriff Hutton to ensure that all was ready there to receive the duke and his household, for he would perform such tasks faithfully and without error, and would not return three days late after emptying his purse in some alehouse or brothel. The same could not be said for every youth in Richard's livery.

However, the matter of the marriage did not arise between them until, one day, out on the fells with their hawks, the moment came. They and their company had had good sport, and now they were on their way back home, relaxed, comfortable, and sufficiently dry-throated to have a pleasant cup of ale on their minds.

'I am glad,' Richard said, surprising himself, 'that you and Bess are at ease with one another.'

Thomas half-turned, to where the girl was riding, a length behind the duchess and stirrup-to-stirrup with Lady Beauchamp.

'There is nothing to dislike,' he said. '|Save that I wish her four years older.'

'Hmm,' said Richard. 'Time will amend that. Look, I don't command you to love her. That would be absurd. But I do charge you always to remember that she is my lady's cousin, and thus mine, and treat her as I expect my kinswomen to be treated. As you shall answer to me.'

'Yes, my lord.'

'Her father was a marquess. And although he fought at Barnet on the wrong side, a good man. Few better. And her sons will carry his blood. Always remember that.'

'I shall. But, Cousin, even were her father a squire of low degree, I should value Bess for what she is. I could not do otherwise.'

'Good. *Very* good. I think I have chosen well for her. That her father would approve, may God assoil him.'

Thomas did not answer that, but he felt his chest swell with pride. This was praise, and praise from this man was worth having. He had learned, during his time at Middleham, that Richard's good opinion had to be earned, that it was not granted to all and sundry. It was no small prize he had won.

*

The day of the wedding dawned. The bridegroom, who had barely slept, sought to ease his nerves by riding out of the castle almost as soon as the gates were open, taking with him his goshawk on a gloved wrist but otherwise alone.

The women of the castle, led by Duchess Anne herself, set about preparing the bride. It was a matter of reassuring her, scrubbing her in the tub, and then dressing her, all of these tasks accompanied by a fair amount of amiable gossip, but none of the bawdy jokes and anecdotes that would have been customary had she been but a little older. Despite this limitation, it was not long before all of them were thoroughly enjoying themselves. Even Bess, who did not much relish the scrubbing of her skin, nor yet the extensive combing of her long hair that everyone seemed to consider necessary, took pleasure in the dressing – for never before had she worn such fine clothes – and in being the centre of attention. Even Lady Warwick, not noted for effusiveness, admitted that the girl was pretty, and that her hair, although mousy in shade and quite unexceptional, had responded well to the brushing and had some very proper curls to display.

Meanwhile, the duke and the men of the household were receiving guests, drinking deeply and enjoying a day of ease. Breakfast was a prolonged affair, comprising fresh bread, vast quantities of oysters, a surfeit of sliced beef and a great indulgence in ale. They were such a merry company that it took some time before anyone noticed that the bridegroom was not among them.

It was Brackenbury who was first to realize that his protégé was not present.

'Where can the lad be?' he mused.

'Probably puking down the privy,' laughed Sir Roger Beauchamp.

'Or praying for mercy in the chapel,' suggested Rob Percy.

They mused upon this for fully three minutes before asking their fellows if anyone had seen Thomas Scrope that morning. No one had.

So they laid the problem before Richard.

'Some of you go and look for the lad,' he ordered. 'He cannot be far.'

It became something of a game. They ran off in various directions, making their cry: *Avaunte assemble, avaunte!* Someone even found a horn to blow.

They looked in all the obvious places, then the less obvious places, and then the most unlikely place, the duchess's solar. The bridegroom was nowhere in the castle.

The joke now fell flat, and they began to look on one another with solemn faces. At last, Brackenbury found a stablelad who claimed that Lord Scrope had taken a horse before first light and ridden out.

This information was laid before the duke, who was not pleased.

'By God's precious blood!' he cried. 'If this lad has made a fool of me – of us all – I shall have his hide.'

Those around him did not doubt it. Richard was rarely roused to anger, but that anger was terrible.

The duchess came sweeping down from her solar, Lady Beauchamp at her heels, to offer her counsel. Anne looked concerned rather than angry.

'This is not in the lad's nature,' she said. 'Besides, where could he go?'

'To Masham?' Richard suggested. 'To hide himself in his castle?'

'Scarcely, I think.'

'We had better be sure.'

'The chances are,' Lady Beauchamp said, 'that Thomas has come by some mischance. If he's out on the fells, it's easy enough to get lost. His horse might be lame. Anything.'

They digested that in silence for a moment.

'In either event, we must not sit here like lackwits,' Richard said decisively. 'We must make a search.'

*

It was Lady Beauchamp who found the stray horse wandering high up on the fells, and called to her husband, who at once used his much louder voice to summon assistance. Together they made a careful survey of the immediate area, and there, lying in a gully between two peat hags, was a white-faced young Scrope who was obviously in some pain.

'I think I've broken my leg,' he forced out, between gritted teeth.

So he had, and that created a problem, for there were no convenient hurdles on which to carry him. Rob Percy, who knew the ground well, rode off to seek out the nearest cottage, in the hope that such an item could be procured. It was a long way off, and all knew it would take some time. Lady Beauchamp, far from the best nurse at Middleham but the best available, organized a primitive splint from men's swords and sundry leather belts. She also despatched her husband to Jervaulx Abbey, where there was a monk who had skill at setting bones, to fetch the fellow to the castle. There, eventually, and after long delay, was Thomas Scrope conveyed, resting on a hurdle brought up by a grizzled shepherd and his son.

It was clear there could be no wedding that day. The monk arrived and dealt with the break, pronouncing it a clean one, and proper splints were applied. The lad was then left to rest in his bed, covered in blankets, having first been fussed over by various broth-bearing females, including Lady Warwick, all of whom had developed a sudden urge to mother him.

'Well, what a mess I have made of it,' Thomas said to Bess, when he woke and found her sitting next to him.

'I'm just glad you are safe,' she said, looking at him with large eyes. 'We can be married when you are well again.'

She was still clad in her wedding finery.

'You are very pretty,' he said kindly. 'And I am very fortunate. We can wait, if you wish, or, if it pleases you, we can be wed tomorrow. They can carry me into the chapel. If necessary, I can say the words lying down.'

She laughed at that, but then smiled and nodded.

So it was agreed, and it proved that neither Higher Authority nor yet the duke's chaplain had any objection. Many smiles and approving nods were occasioned. Even Margaret Beaufort, Lord Stanley's wife, formed her thin lips into her nearest approximation of joy.

The ceremony was, perhaps, unique. The bridegroom was indeed carried to the chapel on a pallet, but, with the aid of several supportive friends, he was able to stand next to his diminutive bride. They said their words, the priest said his, and all was done. The groom's inability to kneel at any point in the proceedings was overlooked.

It also proved possible for Scrope to take his seat at the wedding banquet, although with his leg at an improbable angle and with much gritting of teeth. From time to time, two or three of his fellow squires were required to assist him to the privy, since even a young bladder can only contain so much wine. Dancing, of course, was quite beyond him. He had to be content with watching from a cushioned seat, almost but not quite prone, as the various guests approached him to offer a mixture of congratulations and sympathy. Jokes were made, of course, mainly at his expense, but he laughed along with them and was much admired for his high spirits – even though those high spirits were at least in part due to the duke of Gloucester's supply of excellent wine, which also served to mask much of his discomfort.

It was fully four years before Bess and Thomas could be bedded together. On that occasion, once more, a great consumption of the duke's wine occurred, but much less ceremony, and the bridegroom was careful not to break his leg in celebration.

The young couple often laughed together when they recalled the circumstances of their wedding day, and those who knew them well shared in their laughter. Masham Castle became a very happy home, and as Thomas always treated Bess with great kindness – and indeed love – he never forfeited Richard of Gloucester's favour. Indeed, he and Richard were bound by a fierce devotion that carried both ways. Loyalty bound them.

Author's Note
Thomas, Lord Scrope of Masham remained faithful to Richard all his days, and indeed beyond Richard's death, as he continued opposition to Henry VII for some time after Bosworth. He and Bess were fated not to have a son, but they did have a daughter, Alice, who married Henry Scrope, Lord Scrope of Bolton. His brothers also failed to produce sons, and the line of Scrope of Masham ended in the male line. After Thomas's death in 1493, Bess married Sir Henry Wentworth. She died in 1517 and was buried with Thomas at Black Friars, Ludgate, London.

Some readers may recognize Alianore Audley as the Lady Beauchamp of this story. I could not resist offering her in serious, as opposed to comedy, mode. She and her husband are the only fictional characters mentioned by name in this story, although the events are imagined.

About the author

Brian Wainwright writes in two styles: serious historical fiction, as represented by his Constance of York novels, and comedy/parody/fantasy, as seen in his Alianore Audley novels. Although he has written almost all his life, he is very slow to produce books. His early work was destroyed as not good enough, and more recently he had a long period of illness that left him unable to write anything of substance for more than a decade.

Brian enjoys research. For example, he spent many happy days finding out the correct colour for Garter robes in 1386. Even the Alianore books contain more research than might be thought. However, he is the first to agree that historical fiction can never be one hundred per cent accurate.

Brian's future writing plans include completing the series on Constance of York and possibly another Alianore Audley book. In the longer term, he hopes to write more serious medieval fiction but with a gentler aspect, given that he is rather wearied of bloodshed and politics.

Website: https://sites.google.com/site/brianwainwrightnovels/home
Books: www.amazon.co.uk/stores/author/B001K8RUQS/allbooks

Lovell's Imaginary Boyl and the Mysterious Goat

Susan Lamb

'Lady Anne! Anne!! Anne!!!' We calleth to Oure wyff ... (her name is Anne, thou knowest).

'Twas a Sundaye morn as We stood at Oure oriel wyndowe, wearyng Oure nyte attyre and lookyng acrosse to Muddleham Bridge, when suddenlic We couldst controlleth nott Oure excitement, for We didst espy a myst formationne ... and legges walkyng o'er yon bridge!!

Anne hurryeth in, her curiositie piqued at Oure excitement.

'Oh, Dickon, husband, what ailes thee? Thou hast made me to droppeth one.'

We sniffeth, wrinklyng Oure nose, as she waveth her knittyng at Us ...

'Ah, thy knitting! Oh, ha ha! A dropped stitch, ha ha ...' (Smooths haire down, laughing.) 'Welle, ne'er thee minde thy knitting, dearest, look thee.'

We pointeth. 'Look thee, Anne: Dames!'

'Oh, thy loyalle Dames cometh. How splendid, Dickon! I wonder what they hath brought for thee this time? More of those Jaffa caykes, I suppose ... newe hats ... and those little destrier things, whych I think are a lyttle too young for thee, and that I-runne-brewe, which doth cause unnatural noyses to emerge from thine a-a-assist them acrosse, deare.'

We casteth offe Oure nyte attyre shortes, waveth them, see the Dames faint ... We gaspe! Ohh!! We forgetteth Oureselves! We blusheth, pulle Oure shortes backe on, runne past Anne, whose eyes are now verily shutte tyte, her handes coveryng them. We quicklie don Oure Royalle geare and beste hatt.

We knocketh 'pon Lovell's door.

'Lovell, manne, hurry thee up! 'Tis Oure Dames!'

'Sire! Dickon! Your Grace!'

He unbolteth his door and grabbeth his orange and green hatt, and matching yellow jackette.

'Tastefulle as ever, Lovell,' we commenteth drylie.

A squabble ensues as We doth approach Muddleham Bridge.

'Oh, Oure deare Dames! 'Tis so goodly to see your faces once agayne. Now alloweth Us to taketh your hands as ye steppe acrosse.'

Dames Koko and Jo bycker, as they both reach for Us at ye same tyme.

'No, you went first last tyme. Now it's my turne!'

'No, it isn't!'

'Yes, it is!'

They both grabbeth Us at ye same tyme,

We landeth in a heape, rollyng down ye hillock, Oure suede poulaines wavyng in ye aire, a Dame at each shoulder pullyng Oure hedd left and right, right and left, for kysses!

We rise, smooth Oure haire downe, and brushe at Oure velvett cloak, straighten Oure hatt, wipyng awaye lippie stik from Oure face, as Anne, the minx, watches from her wyndowe, tytteryng!

'Ahem, err, ooh!' We taketh a deepe breath.

'Welcome, Dames, once agayne, to Muddleham. Ye knoweth where your apartements are. So settle ye in, and We shalle see you in the Greyt Hall presentlie.'

We heareth Dame Jo sayeth to Dame Koko: 'Have you got it?'

'What?'

'The goat thinge.'

'Oh, yes, Jo. It's under the Jaffa cake boxe. A bit heaviey, but Lord Lovell will helpe us with it, I'm sure.'

'Aha! Dames!' sayeth Lovell, his eyes twinklyng with mischieffe. 'Woulde ye careth for a gayme of conkers behynde the castle walle?'

'Ah, we will joine thee later, Lord Lovell, but couldst thou assiste us now, for we knoweth thou art awefullie strong!' sayeth Dame Koko.

He puffeth oute his cheste and flexeth his armes.

'Heavens! What is herein?' he asketh, as he lifteth the travelle case.

'Shh! We shouldn't be telling you,' sayeth Jo. 'But the code worde is "goat".'

'What? A goat? Therein? For Ladie Anne's animalle sanctuarie?'

'No, no, not a goat, Sir Francis. We speaketh in code,' sayeth Koko, tappyng her nose.

'Oh, I see!' he sayeth. ''Tis the code of the goat, hmm!' He tappeth his nose also and noddes.

Koko and Jo looke at one another and shrugge.

We walketh into ye Greyt Halle, as a trumpeter blasts offe a fanfare ... Dame Koko jumpes a myle, and Dame Jo snyggers.

Oure Dames curtsey and We wave them to be seated, before they swoone ... Ah it happens so oft with female creatures. We understand it not. Smooths haire downe.

Oure Dames present gyftes to Us: a lovelie crocheted boare from Dame Lynne, who is newe here and a gueste of Dame Koko.

Dames Koko and Jo approacheth Us, lookyng at each other with naughtie smirkes upon theire faces.

Dame Koko speaketh.

'Sire, we will giveth thee one later, in ye courtyarde. Er, that is to saye, 'tis welle worth waityng for and, er ...'

''Tis a surprise,' sayeth Dame Jo.

'Oh, ye naughtie Dames, keepyng your king in suspenders! Then We shalle see ye in ye courtyarde later.' We wynketh, and both swoone.

Suddenlie, Lovell pypes uppe.

'And 'tis not baaaaaad either, Dickon!'

'Lovell, manne, what ailes thee? Thou soundest like a constipated goat!'

'What? Oh, nothinge, Dickon, nothinge at aaaaall!' he bleateth.

We giveth him a funnie looke, and maketh a mentalle note to fetche yon wyse woman from Muddleham Magna. Mayhap he is in agonie with another boyl ... 'Tis the cheese he eates, thou knowest: it causeth awfulle humours resultyng in bigge boyls ... We blame Miss Emm Entalle, overfeedyng him as usualle, obviouslie. (Tut-tuts and frownes.)

Dames Koko and Jo looketh at one another and shrugge.

After Oure Dames are rested and refreshed, wearyng theire beste gownes, we have a Royalle Banquette, a rather casual affaire with bigge fruitie tartes, caykes, cheeses, hammes and nutts. We asketh Dame Koko politelie if she wouldst liketh one of Oure nutts with chocolate on it, and she didst fainte ... We calleth oute:

'Lovell! Mead for the Dame!'

He doeth right funnie lyttl skippes and leapes, and sayeth:

'Right awaaaay, Dickon!' (Shakes hedd and pinches bridge of nose.)

We really must calleth ye wyse woman, for lo! We knoweth now wherest it is! To see him skippyng in this waye, telleth Us 'tis in ye same place as before. He surelie is in payne or he wouldst not walke so verilie strangelie. We must acte quicklie afore the madnesse taketh holde.

We nodd and maketh a decisionne.

We beckon Oure messenger boye, Varys Wiftly, and instructe him to summon ye wyse woman to Lovell, saying that We suspecte a boyl, whych will causeth ye skippyng madnesse if not lanced, for he thinketh he hath turned into a Billie goat.

Then We hath had Oure puddyng, spiced pears

and custard – yum! (Lickes lippes and patts tum.)

Dame Koko and Jo asketh Us to followeth them into ye courtyarde.

'Ye courtyarde, Dames?'

'Oh, yes, Sire. There's somethinge we wysh to unveile,' sayeth Dame Koko.

'Yes, we have somethinge excityng to showe thee, my Liege,' sayeth Dame Jo.

'Oh, ye naughtie Dames! What mischieffe are ye up to? Verilie welle, We cometh.'

Dame Koko taketh Oure hande and sayeth: 'Aye, Sire. We hope thou likest oure gyfte. Ye sculptor didst goeth a lyttl overboarde with the capitalles though, but 'tis Marble of Swaledale, so we cannot change them. However, Jo and I hope thou appreciate oure lovyng thoughts of thee, as loyaltie byndes us.'

We are about to giveth Dame Koko a kyss for such loyaltie, when, at this momente, Lovell appeareth, stycks both thumbs up at Us and does lyttle prances and skippes.

Dame Koko scowles at Lovell, Dame Jo shaketh her hedd.

We cougheth.

'Ahem, Dames. Ignore his temporarie madnesse. 'Tis a boyl. It hath caused a badde humour whych hath affected his braine, and he thinketh he is a goat. We are afraid 'tis in ye same place as laste tyme, when Rufus, Oure hounde, didst, er ... deale with it, and that is ye explanationne for his verilie strange gaite.'

'We remember,' they sayeth, together.

'I wysh we hadn't showne it to him,' sayeth Dame Jo.

'Too late now,' sayeth Dame Koko. 'Especiallie when he has a boyl.'

'No, no, he hasn't got a boyl. He thynks we've got a goat under that sheete, and he's trying to give Dickon subtle clues!'

'Subtle?'

As Oure Dames chunter betweene themselves, We espy Anne, followed by ye wyse woman, holdyng a bigge bodkin.

Standyng in ye courtyarde, We awaite Oure Dames, to unveile Oure surpryse.

'Welle, Dames, We are here. So, without further ado, pulle it offe!'

They looketh at Us with a glazed expressionne.

'Go on, pulleth offe ye cloth, for We are impatiente!'

'Oh, haha! Yes, Dickon, er, Sire,' sayeth Dame Jo.

They unveile a magnificente statue of Us in armoure, on Syrie, whych beareth ye legend:

GREATEST OF ALL TYME
KING RICHARD III OF ENGLAND

We chuckle hertilie, as We standeth backe to looketh.

'Dames, look ye. When standyng farther awaye from it, onlie the capitalles stande oute, and lo, it sayeth GOAT!'

We start to laugheth 'till teares runne downe Oure cheekes. Anne joineth in with ye titteryng Dames. 'Twas funnie, Wethinks.

Suddenlie, Lovell rusheth past. Ah, he runneth normallie agayne, followed by Rufus, who is followed by ye wyse woman, followed by Anne. He yelleth:

'I HATH NOT A BOYL!!'

She yelleth: 'HE HATH!!'

We smirketh in a verilie evil waye.

About the author

Susan Lamb, in the wake of the rediscovery of King Richard's grave and his popularity particularly among women, created the popular 'Dickon for His Dames' Facebook page in which 'Dickon' is alive and well and ruling his kingdom from his beautiful castle of Muddleham. From this sprang the humorous *Dickon's Diaries* books, in which Susan and her co-writer, J. R. Larner, often feature as Dames Koko and Jo.

Susan lives with husband Ray, mom Chris, and sprocker spaniel Duke in the West Midlands, where she enjoys writing short stories, especially ghost stories, and, liking nothing better than to be around horses, is a supporter of Redwings Horse Sanctuary.

.

Books: https://www.amazon.co.uk/dp/B07FK79RSR

The Middleham Jewel

Joanne R. Larner

Richard was excited as he accompanied his mentor, Richard Neville, the earl of Warwick, into York. As he, himself, was still just a squire in the earl's household, despite being the king's brother, he didn't often leave the castle of Middleham to visit York.

They rode into the Alderman's House on Stonegate, one of the most important and prestigious streets in the whole country, leading, as it did, to the impressive York Minster, a monumental building, although still not quite completed. The Alderman's House was home to the new mayor of York, William Snawsell, and his family. Snawsell was also a prominent and respected goldsmith, and it was in this capacity that Warwick was seeking him out today, as he had an important commission for him.

As they and their escort dismounted and their horses were taken to the stables to be rested and fed, a young girl came forward and curtsied. She was richly dressed, in silk and velvet in a fashionable style, and her neck, wrist and several fingers bore large jewels encased in gold settings, even though she looked to be little older than Richard himself, who was twelve. As she rose on Warwick's command, Richard realized she was in fact taller than him, as many girls of his age were. He wished once again that he would soon grow to be as tall as his impressive brother, King Edward IV, who was ten years older than him and almost a foot taller.

He drew himself up to his full height anyway and looked at the girl from the corner of his eye. She had been glancing at him it seemed, for she immediately lowered her gaze and a soft flush spread across her cheeks.

'We are here to see Master Snawsell,' Warwick said, getting straight to the point as always.

'He is my father, my lord,' the girl replied. 'I am Alice Snawsell. I will take you to him immediately, if you care to follow me.'

Warwick nodded, and the girl led them up the outside staircase of the house, which was located at the back of the business premises. Warwick was such an important customer that his visit warranted admittance to the private area of the building. This opened, via a wooden door, into the parlour, where Snawsell conducted important business and kept his most precious treasures, documents and jewels.

As Warwick entered, followed by Richard, a stocky – some might say corpulent – man stepped forward, a beaming smile on his face, his chest weighed down with a gold chain of office and his fingers sparkling as the sunlight struck the expensive jewels he wore on them: rubies, emeralds, sapphires and diamonds. Well, as a goldsmith Richard supposed he had to display his wares and his wealth. The man waved his daughter away, into the house, and she left, throwing a wistful look at Richard, accompanied by a shy smile, before she closed the door behind her.

William Snawsell made a low obeisance to the two visitors and bade them welcome, offering them wine in silver cups and a tray of sweetmeats – honey cakes and marchpane.

'Well, my lord of Warwick, I hear you have a new commission for me,' he said. 'I hope you were satisfied with the goblets I made you last time.'

'They were truly splendid, Snawsell,' Warwick replied. 'You excelled yourself, as usual. Yes, this commission is for a jewel for my wife, as a gift this yuletide. It is a very personal thing, so I hope I can rely on your discretion?'

'Of course, of course,' Snawsell said, nodding his

head vigorously.

Warwick continued, 'As you know, we have two daughters, but no sons – none surviving in any case. I, therefore, want to commission a special jewel, set in a pendant, which needs to open to accommodate a relic or holy object. It must be lozenge-shaped and have a large sapphire at the top, for the Blessed Virgin Mary. Underneath this should be engraved a depiction of the crucifixion and, on the back, another engraving, of the nativity, above an image of the Lamb of God. Around the edge should be depicted fifteen saints. I will let you know which they should be, but please include Saints George, Barbara, Margaret of Antioch, Catherine of Alexandria, Dorothea of Caesarea and St Anne.'

'It will be as you command, my lord,' said Snawsell.

*

One month later, Richard was tasked with collecting the finished jewel from the premises of the goldsmith. He and his small escort of four men-at-arms rode into the courtyard with a clatter of hooves and the girl, Alice, again welcomed him. This time, though, as Warwick was absent, she was a little bolder and spoke more to him, smiling and blushing as she escorted him up to her father's parlour, while the men of the escort made for the kitchens for refreshment. Richard was too young to realize she was rather enamoured of him, but he recognized something different in the way she acted.

She opened the parlour door for him and he entered, removing his hat and nodding his head to the portly man behind the desk in the corner.

'Ah, my lord of Gloucester, I was expecting you,' Snawsell said. He opened a locked drawer and removed a soft leather bag, placing it on the surface in front of him. 'Please take a look to ensure its quality before you take it to the earl.'

Richard opened the bag and gently tipped the contents into his hand, drawing an involuntary breath of wonder at the intricate scenes carved into the gold and the impressive blue sapphire set into the top.

'It is truly wonderful workmanship,' he said, smiling at the goldsmith, who beamed back at him. 'I'm sure the earl will be well satisfied. Er, may I ask you a question?'

'Of course, of course,' replied Snawsell.

'Your name. It is most unusual. I have never heard of anyone else going by that name locally.'

'Ah, yes, we are actually related to the Snowshill family from Gloucestershire, your titular county, my lord. But the local dialect here in Yorkshire has gradually turned it into Snawsell, sometimes even Snozzle!' He laughed.

Richard accepted a goblet of wine while he and Snawsell concluded the business side of the deal.

'You will stay the night, my lord? It is a long journey to undertake twice in one day. Stay and you can join us for our evening meal and leave in the morning after a refreshing and comfortable night's sleep.'

So Richard stayed on as an honoured guest. Snawsell's daughter Alice fluttered her eyelashes at him as he shared a trencher and goblet with her, and he was startled to feel her hand on his knee at one point, though she removed it immediately, acting as if it had been an accident. Richard felt a strange excitement in his stomach at her touch and smiled at her with a little more warmth from then on.

The following day, he collected his men, mounted his horse and set off for Middleham, the precious jewel wrapped in the softest kidskin and tucked into a pouch inside his tunic. The road was long and he and the men stopped on the way to rest and graze the horses and take some small refreshment themselves.

As they continued on their way, they saw a band of riders on the road ahead of them. Richard's men moved so that he was in the centre of their group as they approached. The five strangers seemed respectable enough, although their clothing was neither as rich nor as new as Richard's, and they gave a nod as they passed by. But just as Richard was breathing a sigh of relief, the men turned their horses and, with a whoop, attacked his company from behind.

Swords rang as Richard's men clashed with the brigands. One of the strangers, wielding a large, wooden cudgel, clouted Rob, chief of the guards, knocking him unconscious to the ground. Richard's emotions were mixed as he drew his own sword – partly fear, partly confusion, but mainly anger.

'Ride for Middleham, Your Grace,' hissed Piers, another guard, laying into two of the attackers at once.

Richard hesitated just a second before ignoring his suggestion. Instead, he urged his horse towards Piers and swung his sword at one of the attackers. Although still young, he had been training to fight for many years, since a young boy, when he and his brothers, Edward, Edmund and George, fought 'battles' against each other. Edward and Edmund were older, already trained warriors, so he and George had learned a great deal, later refined under Warwick's tutelage.

Richard's sword struck the assailant's arm – not with full force, but the man cried out, dropped his dagger and rode off, shouting for his gang to follow. In the ensuing chaos, one of the brigands' horses bumped into Richard's, causing it to rear in terror and almost throw him, and him to thank God he was such a good horseman already.

He and his guards regrouped to assess the damage.

'Do you think they were after the jewel?' Richard asked anxiously.

'I shouldn't think so,' said Rob, rubbing his sore head. 'How would they know you were bringing it home to Middleham today? No, I think they were just trying their luck, noticing we are a small band and well-dressed. Luckily, they didn't know you're such a plucky lad, Your

Grace.'

Smiling, Richard thanked him. As they all mounted to set off once more for Middleham, he felt inside his tunic for the pouch.

'Wait!' he cried, dismayed. 'The jewel is gone! How did they get it? The earl will kill me when he finds out.'

'But none of them came close enough to steal it, did they?' said Tommy, another of the company.

'That's what I thought,' Richard replied. 'That's why I was so relieved when they left. But it's gone!'

'Could it have fallen out when your horse reared?' suggested Piers. 'Let's search for it.'

They dismounted again and searched the grass and weeds beside the track while William, the fourth guard, held the horses.

It was Richard himself who found it.

'I've got it!' he called in delight, waving the pouch around.

'You'd better check it's still in there first,' said Rob.

Richard was already opening the pouch and he breathed a sigh of relief at the glint of the golden jewel in the sunlight. What a day! He shuddered as he thought about Warwick's reaction, had he lost the precious gift.

*

Richard's life at Middleham Castle was about to come to an end. His brother, the king, had summoned him to return south after a quarrel with Warwick. The cause was Edward's secret marriage to Elizabeth Woodville, a Lancastrian widow from a family not of the old nobility. Her father was a simple knight, which led to resentment among the established nobles, especially Warwick. The earl wanted his daughters, Isabel and Anne, to marry Edward's royal brothers, George and Richard, but Edward refused his consent. He ordered Richard to leave

Middleham immediately, so his budding romance with Snawsell's daughter was curtailed, before it could even begin.

Meanwhile, the countess of Warwick, Anne Beauchamp, was captivated by the wonderful gift from her husband, never knowing how close it had come to being lost. She wore it on a gold chain around her neck and kept within it a fingernail said to have been that of the Holy Mother, Mary.

Warwick sighed when he heard her praying one day in their private chapel.

'St Anne, who conceived and bore the Holy Mother herself, please grant me the gift of a son.'

She wept while naming in turn each of the saints engraved on the fabulous jewel and ended by beseeching Mary herself and Jesus Christ to bless her and her husband with a son.

'Anne, sweeting!' broke in Warwick. 'It's not going to happen. Don't keep torturing yourself with this longing for a son. I, myself, have long resigned myself and am content with our lovely daughters. Please, wife, cease this constant prayer. You must bear this burden, as must I.'

After a long silence, the countess replied, 'You are right, husband.' She rose to her feet with a deep sigh. 'I am too old now to bear another child. I will do as you say.'

She bowed her head and followed him to the great hall, where they ate their evening meal. Though much music and merriment accompanied the wonderful food, the countess remained sad and ate little. Afterwards, Warwick took the left-over meat to the castle gates, where the poor of the town were waiting. As ever he had ensured he ordered more than his family and household would need, so the poor were always well-served by him.

After retiring to her chamber for the night, Countess Anne wrapped the jewel in its kidskin and returned it to the pouch. She held the precious bundle for a minute or so, before, with another sigh, locking it in a chest. As she said her nightly prayers, a tear escaped, tracing a wet trail down her cheek. She slid into bed and blew out the candle.

*

More than seven years after his departure, Richard rode through the gates of Middleham Castle again as Edward's lord of the north. Accompanied by his new wife, none other than Warwick's daughter Anne, he was light of heart to return to the place where he had been happiest as an adolescent. There was no Warwick to welcome him this time, as he had been killed at Barnet, Richard's first battle. Although Richard was sad things had ended that way for his mentor, he was glad Middleham now belonged to him. He had always felt at home there. It had been expedient for Richard and Anne to marry. She benefited from Richard's protection and he gained further northern lands from her and her inheritance. He was also fond of her, of course. After his interest in girls had been awakened by Alice Snawsell, he had sown his share of wild oats, and at twenty he was ready to settle down and start a family. Where better to make a home than at Middleham?

The couple soon became accustomed to being the lord and lady of Middleham. Richard was head of Edward's Council of the North and, having studied the law under Warwick's tutelage, enjoyed judging local disputes. He deployed the law fairly, passing judgments equally on the rich as on the poor, on the powerful as on the weak. Anne ran the household efficiently, having learned at her mother's knee. Their only regret was that, in the two years following their marriage, Anne had not yet conceived a child.

'Richard,' she said, after another month of failing to do her duty by providing him with an heir, 'I'm a failure as a wife! All I want is to be a mother to your child. Yet God seems to have denied me. Why? What have I done wrong?'

He watched her pretty face crumple as she wept

piteously.

'Do not weep, Anne. There is still time. We are both young and there are many years ahead of us. Try not to obsess over it. You are just distressing yourself, my love.'

He took her in his arms, stroking her silky hair and kissing the top of her head.

'If only I had someone to turn to for advice,' she said. 'There is no one I trust to help. Father John just tells me it will happen "in God's own time", and Hobbes says he can see no reason why I haven't conceived. Even the local wise woman, Old Agnes, has not helped. The little bag of herbs she told me to wear next to my skin has had no effect. Richard, my mother is still in sanctuary in Beaulieu. Could we not bring her to live with us here? Please, my love. I'm sure she could give me advice. It would make me so happy.'

Seeing her eager expression, Richard couldn't refuse. And so, within a few weeks, the countess of Warwick returned to Middleham. Richard smiled when, a few days later, he saw them chatting as they embroidered some kerchiefs and he even caught Anne laughing at some memory the countess had mentioned.

Some time afterwards, he was checking the estate's accounts when he came upon an expense he didn't recognize.

'By God!' he exclaimed, calling his secretary over. 'What is this? Who has spent a fortune on this … this "tablet of gold"?'

'It's the countess, Your Grace,' the man explained. 'She has ordered a golden tablet, a jewel, to be made. I know it is expensive, but you did say she has the freedom to purchase anything she wishes.'

'But hey-ho! Within reason, man! This is a preposterous amount to be spent on a jewel.'

'She says it is for your wife, my lord. To help her conceive. Apparently, the countess had a similar one when she was younger.'

'Snawsell's jewel. Yes, I remember it. But it didn't work! She had no more children after she got the jewel.'

Richard frowned and, dismissing the secretary, marched off to his mother-in-law's solar.

'My lady mother,' he began. 'What is the meaning of this?'

He waved the page containing the offending item.

'Hmm?' the countess said, her thin eyebrows raised innocently. She peered over his shoulder. 'Oh, that! Yes, it's for Anne. To help her conceive, since it seems you can't manage it on your own.'

'But look at the price! It's ridiculous! And don't you already have such a jewel? Why can you not give that to Anne?'

'Because you and your grasping brothers deprived me of all my riches – as if I were dead! And that included the jewel. If you don't have it, then George or Edward does. Don't you want Anne to have your heir?'

Richard took a deep breath and delivered his last argument against her.

'Of course I do. But the jewel didn't work for you, did it?

'That's true, but I found out why not. St Penket. I never had St Penket on mine.'

'Who is St Penket? I've never heard of this saint.'

'Well, St Penket is a saint who is worshipped by dancing. And as soon as Anne has the jewel, we are going to the Rubbing House, the house of worship on Middleham High Moor, to give worship by whirling and dancing.'

'What? Whirling and dancing? And you think this will help Anne to conceive?'

'It's worth a try. One of my serving ladies swears that St Penket helped her daughter conceive, after she went dancing.'

Richard pursed his lips, shaking his head in disbelief.

'Very well, but know that I do not approve of this obscure, whirling saint.'

And he turned on his heel and left the chamber.

*

Several months later, Richard caught Anne weeping again. He had endured his wife and mother-in-law gallivanting off to the moors every week to dance and worship St Penket. Now he decided to put his foot down.

'Enough,' he cried. 'Seeing you upset makes me too sad. Your mother's plan hasn't worked. No more St Penket. No more dancing.'

'I don't need to, Richard,' she sobbed.

'What do you mean?' he asked, perplexed.

'I am with child at last!' she said, a tremulous smile lighting up her face through the glistening tears. 'I'm weeping with joy, not despair. We are going to have a baby. Your heir!'

He wrapped her in his arms, his tears mingling with hers.

'I'm so pleased, Anne. For you, even more than for me. I know what this means to you.'

'Maybe St Penket isn't so bad, after all,' she smiled. 'But I do have a confession to make.'

'A confession? What do you mean?' Richard's mind filled with terrible foreboding. Was the child not his?

'I lost the jewel. The last time Mother and I went dancing. I must have dropped it somewhere. I'm sorry. I know how expensive it was.'

Relieved it was nothing worse, Richard embraced her tenderly.

'Do not worry, my love. It has done its job!'

About the author

Joanne R. Larner became fascinated by Richard III when she saw the Channel 4 documentary 'The King in the Car Park' in February 2013. She researched his life and times and read countless novels, but became fed up because they all ended the same way – with his death at the battle of Bosworth. So she decided to write an alternative history version of Richard's story, adding a time travel element, which became the *Richard Liveth Yet* trilogy. This was followed by a standalone novel, *Distant Echoes: Richard III Speaks*, and several short stories featured in other anthologies, and she has also edited *The Road Not Travelled*, an alternative history anthology.

Website: https://joannelarner.wordpress.com/
Books: https://www.amazon.co.uk/stores/author/B00XO1IC4S/allbooks

Fotheringhay, 1476

Matthew Lewis

Fotheringhay Castle, 30th July

The fires and the innumerable bodies moving about the hall like a swaying forest in a heavy wind make it unbearably hot.

Oh, for the feel of the wind on my face, he thinks. *Even the faintest breath of air in this place.*

Richard is twenty-three years old. He is an honoured guest at this great feast given by his brother, the king. Others have shed their mourning clothes in favour of bright colours to enjoy the king's generosity. Edward himself glows in cloth of gold and Yorkist murrey as though he were the fire at the centre of the room. Perhaps, Richard thinks, that is what Edward is. The fire of York. He burns brightly in the eyes of those around him. The heat he emits attracts those seeking to warm themselves but warns too of the dangers of getting too close. This evening, his light is used to blind the world.

'Brother.' The voice, harsh as the ring of metal on metal, is instantly familiar as the breathless frame collapses into the chair beside him.

'George,' he acknowledges sombrely. He really isn't in the mood for this. He forces a smile on to his face, but it comes out lopsided.

'Determined to be the life and soul of the party, as usual, I see.'

Richard looks around the room. Great, long tables are smothered with more food than the guests could ever eat. Yet they try. Throughout the day, thousands have availed themselves of the king's generosity and taken as much home as they could carry. As the wine flows and the volume rises, Richard feels lost. His gaze falls on George, who throws a chicken bone on to Richard's plate, a greasy smile spreading across his face.

'Still acting like a five-year-old, as usual, I see,' Richard grumbles, unable to summon the energy to be annoyed, even by George.

'It's a party, little brother,' the elder taunts. 'Raise a smile.'

'This is a funeral, as you well know.' Richard shoots the other an irritated glare. George is a few years older than Richard and never allows him to forget it. He has the good looks and easy charm of their oldest brother, the king, but somehow, in George, they are all jagged corners that seek to slice fingers where Edward's are smooth. The light that radiates from Edward is all dancing shadows behind George's eyes.

'For people dead fifteen years or more.' George's smile drops. 'Mourned and missed long ago.'

Richard sees the sadness in the depths of his brother's eyes. Another might miss it easily, but Richard knows him too well. Their years growing up together forged something between them. It had proved unbreakable, even amidst George's betrayal and their arguments over the inheritance of their wives.

'I still miss them,' Richard muses, knowing he does so as much to needle George as because it happens to be true. He revolves his wine cup slowly in his hand.

'Mmmm,' George grunts and reaches to select a slice of mutton from a dish. He nibbles at the edge as though he doesn't really want it.

'You got to know them better than I.'

'Barely,' George tells his piece of meat gruffly. 'Father was often away, Edmund even more so.'

Somehow, there is solace in that for Richard. He feels less alone in the grief that has gripped him these past days. He had travelled south from Pontefract to Fotheringhay escorting the bodies of their father and

Edmund, a brother younger than Edward but older than George. Both had been killed on the cold, hard earth at the battle of Wakefield in the winter of 1460. A bitter chill had hung over the family, even as the heat of Edward's rage had blazed in vengeance as though it sought to quench itself in blood. The iciness of their bodies, buried as vanquished enemies, away from home and family, was a shadow conspicuous in the sunlight of Edward's kingship. He had taken what his father had prepared for him, and, finally, the time had come to repay the favour.

'If you don't feel as though you knew them,' George frowns, in his distracted way, as though their conversation was intruding into something more important, 'why ask to bring them here? Why beg Edward to let you do it?'

'I didn't beg.' Richard rises to the bait, as he always seems to do. 'I asked, and Edward gave me the honour. I asked because I wanted to pay my respects to two men who died for all we have today. We live this life because of them. That is worthy of thanks, even if I don't remember them well.'

'Father always had a soft spot for you.' A grudging concession from George. 'He would pick you up and throw you in the air when I was too big. You got his name, and you were also their baby.' He mewls the last word, and the moment of fraternal tenderness is gone.

The barb misses its mark. Richard is smiling. He skewers a piece of pie with his knife, and the pastry crumbles into his lap as he eats it, lost in thought. After a moment, he breaks his reverie, a frown crossing his brow.

'Why didn't you ask?'

'What's the point?' George shrugs, cramming more meat into his mouth so that grease slides down his chin.

'To show respect, and reverence, and gratitude.'

Richard is bemused by his brother's casual response. Having just spent more than a week travelling with their father's and brother's bodies on their final journey, the sneering cuts deeply. Doubtless, it was meant to.

'What's the point?' George repeats. The flash in his eyes tells Richard his brother knows his teasing has roosted well. 'I pray for them, as we should, but this,' he waves a hand around the packed, noisy hall, 'this is all for show.'

'Do you really not care that father and Edmund are home, at rest, at peace?' Richard looks away, trying not to let George see he is sulking.

'Richard.' The patronizing tone drips like the grease on his chin 'They've been at peace for a long time. There's nothing to gain from what you've done. Is this some sense of loyalty to father?' He barely waits for an answer. 'If you want my advice—'

'I sense I won't.'

George ignores the interruption.

'Save your concern for the living. The dead can give you nothing and get you nowhere.'

'Not everything is about what we can gain,' Richard counters.

'Isn't it?' George asks, still maintaining his casual distraction from his brother. 'At least you can trust the dead, I suppose.'

'George!' Richard admonishes. 'You are hardly one to talk about trust or loyalty.'

Though it was years since George threw in his lot with their cousin Warwick to eject Edward from his throne ... George had wanted a crown for himself but scurried back to Edward's side when the wind changed. Yet, no one was quite sure he had lost the notion of becoming a king. A feast, once tasted, will make plainer fare seem duller still.

'Trust?' George retorts, the shadow of his easy anger lowering over his face. He looks suddenly cruel as he drains his cup and slams it back on the table. 'I could no more trust another man than cut my heart from my body and place it in his hand. By design or negligence, he will forget to keep it beating. Why take the risk?'

'Is your opinion of the world so low, brother?'

'It is.'

'And of me, too?'

'Where were you when Warwick would have made me king, and Edward was driven out?'

'Watch your words.' Richard casts an eye around to make sure no one has heard George's treason.

'Where were you?' George's eyes swim a little. Whether it is a reflection of the fire, the drink or a tear, Richard cannot tell.

'You know where I was.' Richard hushes his voice. 'I was with Edward. And you know what you did was wrong.'

'Yes, yes.' George waves his words away in a manner that suggests the wine is taking hold. 'Bad George,' he mocks, his lip curling into a sneer. 'Proves my point, though. I can't even trust my own little brother.'

Richard can think of no answer that isn't the beginning of a fight. It was the kind of comment that doesn't want an answer anyway. He is saved from trying to find one by George, who rises from his seat, sways a little, props himself on the back of a chair for a moment, then looks around the room as if he has forgotten where he is.

'I heard Ned has some of his good Malmsey wine somewhere,' he says to no one in particular, before stomping off again.

George's take on the world is something Richard has not yet managed to untangle. He hates it, believes it is out to get him, yet wants it for himself all at once.

Richard takes a slow sip from his cup and looks around the room. People are crammed into the great hall of Fotheringhay's castle. Tables stretch out along the room, each looking as though it creaks under the weight of food. When something is taken, servants replenish it immediately. It feels oppressive, and Richard is thinking of leaving quietly, when he senses someone sit down in the chair beside him. He turns to see, then stands so quickly he almost knocks his own chair flying.

'My lady!'

'Oh, Richard,' a familiar voice chastises him, softened by a smile. 'Sit down. I'm your mother, and this is a party.'

'Yes, mother.' He gently retakes his seat.

'How are you?'

'Do you mean to ask what George wanted?'

'No.' The smile is gone, leaving only the censure. 'Your days have been long and hard to return your father and Edmund home. To me.'

'It was my honour, my lady.'

'Your father would be proud.'

Does she know how he has yearned to hear those words? How long he has hoped they might be true? Has she seen the hole within him he has filled in recent days?

'I am proud of you too, Richard.'

He smiles. 'But you would like to know what George is up to?'

'It is dangerous not to,' his mother tells him softly, but she is smiling again too.

'He sees little benefit in all this.' Richard waves a hand at the festivities surrounding them. 'He trusts no one but himself.'

'So, he is still George, then.'

'You are not surprised?'

'By George?' His mother leans towards him with a conspiratorial look. 'Not in a long time. The benefit here is to the crown, to Edward, to the family. Because it is not of direct consequence to George, he sees no use in it.

'Sometimes I feel I know him,' Richard muses. 'Yet often he seems like a stranger.'

'He was born in Dublin, and is a lot like Ireland. He is close, yet distant. He can appear to follow the rules but play his own games when no one can see. His public oaths do not necessarily control his private thoughts.

Understanding his lawlessness is the only hope of containing it.'

'You paint a dark picture of your son.' Richard frowns. Does she speak of him like this to others? He hopes not.

'He is full of darkness.' Cecily looks away, hoping to prevent a tear from escaping her eye. It has been an emotional day, leaving her ill-equipped for these kinds of thoughts. Painting on a smile, she looks back to Richard. 'It's a mother's curse – to try to nurture the light we will always see.'

There is a long silence between them, only partly pierced by the hum of a hundred voices and the thrum of music. Richard thinks of the past eight days, escorting two coffins and an effigy of his father to this place. The long, sombre days in the saddle. The evenings at prayer in churches where the cortege rested, unbearably hot in the blaze of myriad candles. The nights of fretful sleep as thoughts beyond his control plagued his dreams.

'What do you see in me?' he asks.

'My baby,' Cecily replies, her eyes refocusing on him.

'I'm twenty-three.' He blushes a little.

'Twenty-three, married, a great lord.' Cecily pinches his chin. 'And still my baby.'

Her thumb finds the groove in his chin, and a flood of warm emotion courses through her.

'You are so much like him.' Her voice is distant, tinged with sadness. Her hand falls away.

'I'm sorry. I wish I didn't cause you such pain.'

'Motherhood is pain.' She looks away, then returns her gaze to him, a happier expression upon her face. 'This is a pleasant kind.'

'What pain is it Edward causes you?'

He regrets the sullen question as soon as it leaves his lips. He may be most like their father, but Edward is her golden boy.

'More than you can know,' she replies, without

meaning to, then deftly changes the subject, a quick smile covering her lapse. 'George trusts no man, and your father trusted too many too easily. Where will you put your marker?'

He shrugs. 'Carefully.' He hates tests, particularly ones he suspects he's supposed to fail.

He is too much like his father, not just in looks, for her to believe him. But she believes he thinks he means it. She flashes him a bright smile.

'My father always taught me that family was everything. Mind you, he had two families, and his first might not feel he upheld that sentiment in their regard. My mother brought royal blood, and he found his second family held more opportunity than the first.'

'Perhaps I see where George gets it from,' Richard says quietly, but not quietly enough. He sees the look his mother shoots him.

'I wish you were wrong,' she concedes, then continues seriously. 'Family must be your keystone. You have proved yourself a worthy son of York. Edward has secured what your father won. He will need you, and you will need him. Do not let George ruin it all.' She fixes him with a piercing stare few could hold for long. 'Be true to family.'

They lock eyes a moment, and the noise of the room falls further away. Cecily reaches out and gently places her palm on Richard's cheek.

'You are so like him.'

She smiles again, but Richard sees the pain in her eyes and knows he is the cause of it. He is a constant reminder of her loss.

As Cecily, pulling her hand away, rises from her chair, so does Richard. He bows his head, partly in deference but more to avoid seeing the hurt carved upon her face. She doesn't mean it, he knows, but still …

He watches her leave before sinking back into his seat and reaching for his cup. He takes a long draught as if it might dull his prickly thoughts. When he puts the cup down again, a smiling boy, scurrying around with a large jug, refills it without looking at him.

'My thanks,' Richard says absently, then locating some bread upon the table, tears off a hunk and tosses a small piece into his mouth. As George is prone to demonstrate, too much wine without enough food is a recipe for trouble.

A movement of air behind him causes him to tense. With a thud, someone new takes the seat beside him. He doesn't need to look up. Smiling, he welcomes the newcomer.

'Your Grace.'

'Little brother,' comes the gleeful reply. Edward, like George, is deep into his cups. Unlike George, it makes Edward happier, and he can handle the amount he drinks.

'Would you know what George wanted?' Richard asks. Even in his state of inebriation, Edward will have been watching George tonight.

'I can probably guess.' Edward returns his smile, then sets his face in imitation of a crying baby. 'Wah, wah, life's not fair, wah, Edward's mean, nobody loves me, wah wah.'

Richard splutters in laughter. Edward has done this impression a great deal since their father's death. When they were children, George was a constant in Richard's life, but being a few years older meant that sometimes he was abrupt. Or just plain cruel. Edward was the only one who seemed to see it, and his impression of George, which makes him the baby of the family, always lands well with Richard.

'How did I do?' Edward takes a long drink from his golden cup.

Only after being away from his brother for a time does Richard appreciate what others see in him. To Richard, he is the big brother who filled the space left by their father. He has protected Richard and delivered security into his life when none has seemed to be in sight. Edward grew up with Edmund at Ludlow, long gone from the family home when Richard was born. His first memory of Edward was seeing him sparring in the outer bailey of Ludlow Castle sixteen years or more ago.

Richard watched a man wearing only half his armour taking on all comers. Towering above them, he struck them with an easy power that was terrible for the seven-year-old Richard to behold. He was taller than any man in the castle and emitted an infectious energy; even those he knocked down seemed to enjoy it. In that instant, that was what Richard wanted to be. When the man loped over and introduced himself as Richard's big brother, the boy's chest filled with hope that he really could be like that. Yet, with the curving of his spine as he reached his teenage years, it became obvious that it was not to be.

'Impeccable, as ever.'

Richard smiles at Edward's glowing face. He is warm from dancing and has taken some of the colour of his rich red wine into his cheeks.

'Good to know I'm not losing my knack,' his brother grins. 'Besides, I might as readily ask what mother wanted. You two looked as thick as thieves.'

'She is melancholy.' Richard's eyes fall. This is Edward's fear of the family their mother promotes as safety. George has betrayed him. Being family earned him forgiveness, but Edward cannot forget. He cannot afford to forget. And so, he sees the shadows of plots where there are none. It is hard to blame him, but harder for Richard to be on the receiving end of his suspicions.

'Yes.' Edward softens a little. 'I should have guessed. I was eighteen when our father and Edmund died. I barely knew him, but you—'

'I'm just like him,' Richard cuts in to finish the sentence. They share a smile.

'All of this is for them, and she sees what she lost alive in you. It's a source of sadness but also of more comfort than you can imagine.'

Edward is uncharacteristically serious. Richard wonders whether he has finally discovered an amount that constitutes too much wine for his huge frame.

'I'm doing all of this,' Edward waves a hand around the heaving, hot room, 'for them and for us.'

'Mother was telling me all about family and how I should place my faith in mine.' Richard has no desire to allow his brother, his king, to think he is hiding things. That path is dark and dangerous.

'God's teeth!' Edward curses with a laugh. 'She must be melancholy.'

'You think she is wrong?'

'Have you met George?' The king laughs once more, but there is no mirth in his face.

Richard turns in his chair to face him. 'Then what am I to do?'

Edward swigs from his cup. 'Family is a fine idea', he says, 'but it's full of people, and they're the problem. You know the story of William Marshal?'

'Of course.' Richard perks up at mention of such a chivalric figure, who served five kings three centuries earlier, becoming regent for the young King Henry III. He appears in some of Richard's favourite books.

'Marshal perfected the art of serving the crown without concerning himself with who wore it.'

'You think he is a good example for our family?' Richard asks, casting his eyes around the room. 'We are here because our family acted against old King Henry and because that cost father and Edmund their lives.' He sees Edward wince at Edmund's name. They were close, and Richard knows he still misses a boyhood friend, frozen forever in his mind at the age of seventeen.

Edward ignores the comment. 'We are the royal family now, and the crown can be your focus.'

'Not you?' Richard asks with a frown.

'Yes, me, but not just me.' Edward leans towards him. 'My son will be the next king, and you and he may not get on. Your son and his might not get on. Personality is dangerous. It can bind men together or drag them apart.

The crown is a constant, bigger than any man who wears it.'

Richard considers Marshal, a man who managed even to serve King John. Edward is making a powerful point.

'I hope we will never have to divide family from friendship and from the crown,' he thinks aloud.

'So do I, but hope is a fragile thing.' Edward takes another long swig, then grins broadly. 'My son might be an obnoxious little twerp, like George, but I'd still have you serve him as long as he is king.'

'And I would have that too,' Richard replies earnestly.

'A toast, then.' Edward raises his cup, and Richard reaches for his. 'The crown!'

'The crown, and Your Grace's health!'

Richard sips his wine as he watches Edward drain his cup. From nowhere, a boy appears with a jug to refill it.

'Good, brother.' Edward rises like a man who has drunk no wine for days. 'Best get back to showing these people why they want me as their king.'

He strides away, slapping men on the shoulder, shaking hands, a broad smile across his face and his cup always steady in his left hand.

Richard takes another sip. All these people are here to remember the lives of men some never knew. It feels unseemly, until Richard remembers he might be counted among those who barely knew the two. Still, at least he is family. Many are here so that the king knows they are here. More have come for the free food.

A hand alights gently on his shoulder, pulling him from his thoughts. The familiar touch sends a warm sensation through his body and his face lights up. His wife walks behind his chair towards that vacated by Edward. Richard rises, retaking his seat only as she lowers herself into hers. She is nearing halfway through her pregnancy now. Though no sign of her swelling stomach can be seen beneath her skirts, Richard has noticed her moving more gingerly in recent weeks.

'Do you wish to retire?' he asks, hoping for an excuse to leave.

'No,' Anne replies softly. 'You have worked hard for this reward.'

'None of this is for me,' he says, mirroring her smile. 'It is for father and Edmund. And you know I hate this sort of thing.'

'Do you not wonder why Edward is doing this now?'

Anne's question is the kind Richard recognizes now. She has wisdom to dispense.

'France was a mess. This is overdue and offers a good excuse for a huge party.' Yet he knows she will have more to say.

'All true,' she says, her tone conspiratorial. 'Edward raised a great deal of money for the invasion of France, only to be bought off by more great sums. This is overdue, though your brother hardly needs an excuse to eat and drink plenty.'

They exchange an amused look. 'But there is more?' he asks.

'There is always more.' Anne sometimes sounds like a disappointed tutor. 'There was a,' she pauses, as if trying to select a word, 'an accident on the way home from France.'

'To my lord of Exeter?' Richard hushes his tone again. 'Everyone knows it is unlikely to have been an accident, but God forgive me, he had it coming. He was vile to our sister Anne.'

'He was, for a time, your brother-in-law.'

Richard frowns. 'And a constant foe to my family despite it.'

'So were many other men, some here tonight.'

'What is your meaning?' He is a little lost, which he suspects is Anne's plan.

'If Holland did not die by accident, it was not his

loyalty in battle that condemned him, but the blood in his veins – spilled so freely at Barnet five years ago, and yet he survived.'

'I faced Exeter that day,' Richard is even more confused.

'And flanked him with ease. Do you think *that* was an accident?'

'We were misaligned in the fog,' Richard recites. Barnet saw Anne's father, the earl of Warwick, killed fighting against Edward and Richard. He knows it is a cause of some pain for his wife.

'If the fog was to blame,' she whispers. They are deep in their own secret world amidst the noise and levity. 'I wonder whether Edward meant it to happen. One man was intended never to leave that field, and I do not think it was my father.'

'Exeter?' Richard hisses after a moment's thought.

'A great-great-grandson of Edward III. You focus on George as Edward's greatest problem, or my father.' Her eyes lower involuntarily. Only for an instant. Still, Richard spots the sadness. 'But Edward sees greater threats he would destroy. Exeter was meant to die at Barnet. Nearly did die – was believed dead. Plunging into the sea on the way back from France was the end of a fall that should have claimed him five years ago.'

Richard leans back in his seat. What she says makes sense. It usually does. Like her father, she has a sharp mind for politics and sees games that remain invisible to Richard.

'All of this,' Anne continues as she sees her point find its mark, 'is part of Edward's fear. He honours your father as a king by right, if not in fact, because then he is the second king of his dynasty, not the usurping first. He is the fifth Henry, not the fourth. He is the unifier, not the divider.'

'I think you give Edward too much credit.' Richard's frown deepens.

'I think you give him too little.' She smiles. 'He

can achieve more than one thing at once. He honours your father and brother, but builds walls around himself in doing so.'

Richard exhales a long, slow, thoughtful breath.

'George tells me I'm a fool for trusting anyone but myself. Mother, that family is all. Edward, that the crown is more important still. And you see this whole other world that I cannot discern.'

'Loyalty is something we cannot grasp,' Anne's voice is soft, but her gaze is iron. 'It is a wisp. You must be loyal to yourself. Your family is the crown, your brother the head of it, whatever your mother might think, and he is the king too. You hold a position few men have. The king's younger brother. It brings privilege and risk, and it will always demand compromises of you.'

'How am I to deal with all of that?'

'You must listen to your heart, Richard, for it is the best part of you.'

'Perhaps I should just listen to you.'

'Of course you should. You must balance all these things, like jugs of wine on that tray.' She inclines her head, and Richard sees a young man dodging between and around people unaware of his existence, yet managing not to spill a drop of what he is carrying. 'You will see moments when it is clear, you will feel when it is right. Listen with care. Do as your heart tells you.' Her smile broadens. 'And as I tell you, of course.'

'Of course.'

Richard has done much thinking over the past nine days. He sees in Anne's face a constant wariness. Perhaps it is from bearing their first child. Maybe it is the experiences and losses she has endured to this day. Looking at her eyes as they survey the room, Richard sees her slight frown, as though she is calculating something. Perhaps, for all his thinking, he has missed what really matters. His mind meanders through thoughts of the past and strays into the future. What that future might hold remains beyond his knowledge, but he will strive to understand the world Anne sees so clearly, in order to better meet the undoubted challenges that still lie ahead of them.

About the author

Matthew Lewis is an author, historian and podcast host who also presents and appears in documentaries. His main areas of focus are the Wars of the Roses, Richard III and the Princes in the Tower, but he has also written about the Anarchy, Henry II and Eleanor of Aquitaine, and Henry III. Matt co-hosts History Hit's Gone Medieval podcast and hosts the Echoes of History podcast which explores the history behind the Assassin's Creed game franchise. He has recently presented documentaries on Richard III and on the Peasants' Revolt, and is a frequent speaker at events.

Website: https://www.mattlewisauthor.com/
Books: https://www.amazon.co.uk/stores/Matthew-Lewis/author/B0088LP1H0

Confinement

Alex Marchant

He has seen them often. The lions of the Tower – in his brother Edward's menagerie in London. As they pace – up and down, up and down – in their iron cages. The sturdy bars confining them.

But never before has he understood their plight. Their desperation to be free – to move unconstrained by four walls.

Until this day, this night. Shut up as he is in this small tower room. Waiting.

He paces. Up and down. Up and down. Thinks to knock. But no. What use would it be? None will come. Not now. Not to him. He must face this alone.

Alone. Trapped.

He – who is used to galloping free upon the moor, an eager hunting party at his back. Or striding into a packed court room, to sit, to judge – perhaps to send some felon to confinement such as this. Or riding into battle, stout companions at his side, ready to face whatever, whoever, lies ahead.

Bright banners whipping in the wind, throbbing beat of the drum, the tramp, tramp, tramp of many booted feet in lockstep behind, the clash of steel on steel, the cries – warlike, fierce, desperate, forlorn …

The cries. The screams. The battle. The fight.

Beyond the door. Beyond the stone walls. The fight ongoing. The fight that others wage. While he … waits. Confined.

Where is Francis Lovell at this, his time of need? Rob Percy? Old companions both, in pleasure and in war. Why are they not here?

Yet … no … he has forbid them. He had forgot. Said he must be alone.

Alone. Confined.

He paces up and down, up and down the small chamber.

Like the lions.

Lions roar against their imprisonment. He will not roar.

How long now will it be? It seems so long since last he saw a friendly face. So long since this siege began. Since he folded his wife in his arms to comfort her. Her body – fragile, too fragile surely for what was to come. Yet always, always, she had laughed.

'I am a woman, Richard. We are stronger than you think!'

A tap at the door. So soft he could have missed it – had he slept. But sleep has not come. Not this day. Not this night.

He springs to the door. Beyond, a woman. Dressed all in black. But … a smile.

He looks down. A bundle in her hands. Wrapped close, firm, against the chill spring air.

White cloth. Small ruddy face. Eyes closed tight. Quiet now. Breathing softly.

Lifted up – towards him.

'Your Grace. Your child. He is born.'

Thanks be to God!

'A son. Your heir. His mother is well. What shall his name be?'

No hesitation.

'Edward,' he says, taking the tiny body in his arms. 'His name shall be Edward.'

Author's Note
'Confinement' was written during the UK's first Covid-19 pandemic lockdown in spring 2020, in response to a request for a short story to be included in a charity anthology in support of

Médecins Sans Frontières, Yorkist Stories, *edited by Michèle Schindler. Although my time was mostly taken up with family, work and continuing my third book in the Order of the White Boar sequence,* King in Waiting, *I discovered writing a piece of flash fiction about the birth of King Richard's son provided an outlet for some of the frustrations of being confined for the greater good!*

The Investiture

J. P. Reedman

King Richard stepped from the vast, incense-heavy vaults of York Minster into the brightness of the September day. The sun dazzled his eyes and gilded him with its rays, which glinted on his crown and bejewelled collar, making him appear, briefly, as a man wrought of flame, almost otherworldly in his brilliance.

Dark blots silhouetted against the intense brightness, the people of York cheered and waved their new king – hundreds of them, from babes to greybeards, filling the narrow alleys and lanes around the stony feet of the Minster.

The excited babble of their voices swelled over Richard in an intoxicating wave. His brother Edward had been the Sunne in Splendour once, magnificent and terrible, while he and George were two lesser suns at his side, basking in reflected glory. Now, like the sun itself, he had risen to the same dizzying pinnacle as his elder brother – anointed by the holy chrism, the crown of his ancestors on his brow.

And these people, his people of York, approved wholeheartedly; they had none of the doubts he had met with in the south. Not that those whispers had stopped the southern barons from attending his coronation feast – the best-attended such banquet since scribes started recording the event! He thought back to the days, years ago now, when York had been a nest of Lancastrians – with his father's and brother's heads spiked on Micklegate. Its citizens had even acted warily when he and Edward returned from exile in Burgundy. But when he had taken up position in Middleham Castle, he had gradually won the people to his side – although that had not gone down especially well with certain northern lords, in particular his kinsman, Henry Percy, earl of Northumberland. Doubtless Percy felt his toes were being stepped on, since his family had long been considered masters of the north.

'Richard? The bishop is ready to leave.'

The quiet voice of his queen, Anne, broke through the king's musings. He glanced away from the sun's blinding brightness, and as his vision adjusted he saw, beneath the glint of her crown, the white oval of Anne's face, too thin and pale these days but always fair in his eyes. Edward, their only son, stood beside her. He looked slightly bewildered and as if he wished to take her hand. But Edward knew this was the most important day of his short life thus far, and he was trying to assume the gravity of a prince.

As well he might, and this day, truly, was Edward's, not his. Richard smiled down at the boy. Today, during the banquet in the archbishop's palace, he would officially invest his son as prince of Wales. He had already created him prince at Nottingham several weeks ago, but now would raise him to that dignity in glorious splendour, witnessed by men of the church and various lords, barons and dignitaries. He wished that the archbishop himself could have officiated, but Thomas Rotherham had proved false, unlawfully handing the Great Seal over to Elizabeth Woodville and thereby nailing his colours to the Woodville mast. Bishop Dudley from Durham had been a worthy replacement.

'Come,' the king said, nodding in Edward's direction. 'Your mother is right. Time is passing. It would be rude of us to keep the bishop and the dean waiting … although the blame lies fully on my shoulders.' He gave a little laugh. 'I was daydreaming awhile, like one moon-mazed, remembering how things were here years ago.'

Edward blanched white with nervousness, and glanced from his father to his mother. 'Do you think they'll like me? The people, that is. And Bishop Dudley too. He looked so stern and tall.'

'Do not be fearful.' Richard bent low towards the little boy. 'Tonight's celebration is for you. It is a special day that you will remember all your life. These townsfolk are here for you as much as me. And yes,' he gave the child his warmest smile, 'you may take your lady mother's hand as you did when we first entered York. You are yet young, and there is no shame in it.'

Colour returned to Edward's cheeks and he stretched out his hand to Anne, who took it in her own.

'There, we are ready to proceed,' she said, gazing fondly at Edward. 'Let us go, my little princeling. Feasting and friends await!'

The royal party moved from the steps of the Minster, shielded from the sun by a raised canopy of blue silk stitched with suns and stars.

The archbishop's palace was not far away, just beyond the cloister, and soon Richard, Anne and Edward were being escorted by the steward to the dais in the great hall. There they would sit in majesty, surrounded by burning candelabra, the king and queen wearing their crowns, the bishop's great salt cellar, fashioned into a sailing ship, resting on the linen-draped table that stretched before them.

The hall itself was lit by unnumbered candles and the walls hung with imported Flemish tapestries bearing scenes of the Passion and the Annunciation that stretched from floor to ceiling. Shadows danced across the hammerbeam roof, making the carved shield-bearing-angel supports seem to leer, smile or grimace at the activities taking place below.

A clarion called out a clear note, making the occupants of the hall fall instantly silent – the nobles in their jewelled livery collars, the town officials clad in their best gowns, and the high-ranking clergy, such as Bishop Dudley, the dean Robert Booth, the treasurer, the archdeacon, and a swarm of various prebendaries, parsons and vicars.

Richard rose from his seat so all could see him. A sword was in his hand, its blade glinting in the torchlight. Young Edward had been standing to one side near the bishop's throne while his parents sat on chairs of estate under a cloth-of-gold canopy. Now, as Richard gave him an almost imperceptible nod, the boy stepped forward, candlelight gleaming on his dark blonde hair, making it glow around his head like a saint's halo.

Edward knelt before his father, head bowed, clearly nervous. He had practised this move with his tutor for days but was still afraid it would not 'look right'.

Gazing down at the kneeling child, Richard thought about how small he seemed, how fragile, and suddenly it was as if the breath was being squeezed from his own lungs. God had raised him to great heights – but there was always a price to pay. Great responsibilities now lay on his shoulders, but also on the narrow shoulders of the young boy before him. *Edward, Edward, what have I done?*

He fought back the unexpected, sudden sensation of near-panic, and steeled himself to do what he must. The hand of destiny had touched him and his family, and he could not retreat into the past. Those days were gone. He could only move forward, and although little Ned would no longer have a life free of cares, one day, he would be a king.

God willing ...

He brought down the sword, a falling star, for the accolade, touching it lightly on each of his son's shoulders. Then Edward rose, careful not to rush and overbalance, and Richard turned to address the hall.

'We have determined to honour our dearest firstborn son, Edward, whose outstanding qualities give undoubted hope of future uprightness, with grants, prerogatives, and insignia of prince and earl. We do create him prince of Wales and earl of Chester. And we invest him, as is the custom, by the girding on of the sword, the setting of the garland on his head, and placing the gold ring on his finger and the staff of gold in his hand, to have and hold to him and his heirs, kings of England, forever.'

Richard then took up a sheathed sword brought to him by Francis Lovell and buckled it around Edward's waist. A wreath of gold leaf was carried up to the dais on a purple cushion, and this the king lifted on high before setting it carefully on his son's brow. A golden ring and wand of office followed, also borne in upon tasselled cushions – the ring slipped on to the outstretched hand, which the king squeezed conspiratorially, making Edward smile and look more at ease, despite all the eyes upon him.

Richard stepped back, and Edward was alone before the assembled throng, the wand gleaming in his hand, the leaves of the wreath flame-bright upon his brow.

'God save the prince of Wales!' someone shouted from the back of the chamber, and the cry was taken up and repeated, rising to shiver the rafters with their carved faces of angels.

The prince sat down then, on the dais beside the queen, but the knighting ceremony was not yet over. Other youths were waiting to receive their spurs on this grand occasion. First was Edward of Warwick, the son of George of Clarence, Richard's brother who had been executed for treason. A timid pale-faced boy, he was a little younger than Prince Edward and not unlike him in appearance, which was hardly surprising since not only did the two boys have two brothers as their fathers, their mothers were sisters, too.

Edward of Warwick knelt as his cousin had done and Richard graced him with the accolade, then he was led by an attendant to a bench at his allotted table. Several other boys and young men came forward to receive their knighthoods, and finally the king was approached by his natural son, John of Gloucester, born when Richard was only seventeen to a maid from Pontefract called Alice. He had some of the look of his dead uncle, King Edward, about him, being tall for his age and of much heavier build than his father. Richard was deeply proud of him, his firstborn, and envisioned a high future for him someday.

The king's eyes shone with paternal pride as John knelt before him to accept the accolade and his spurs.

With the knighting ceremony over, Richard returned to Anne and little Edward on the dais. Musicians began to play and servants carried in platters heaped with delectable food – *salats* tossed with marigolds; quails, larks and pheasants; pottage of *blandesoure*, a white soup; jellied brawn of a deer.

Francis Lovell, taking on the role of the king's most honoured servant, stepped forward holding a fabled alicorn, a sharp horn fallen from the brow of a unicorn, in preparation to taste the king's food. Having consumed a mouthful of each dish, he pronounced all was well and the feasting could commence.

The banquet lasted a full four hours, finishing with a third course of roasted coneys, bream slathered in mustard, long *frittours* sprinkled with dates, <u>*bruete*</u> of almonds, rich with honey and eggs, and a stewed *lumbarde* of sweet syrup. Lastly, a subtlety was brought from the kitchens and presented to Prince Edward. Of red and white jelly and shaped like a crown, it was decorated with gold foil, from a distance making it look like real gold.

A server cut through the jelly with a knife and Edward ladled it on to his platter. He looked tired now, his eyes underscored by darkness. It had been a long and emotional day for him, a day when he was no longer a duke's son, staying quietly in Middleham with his governess, Anne Idley, while his father was away and his mother occupied with household duties, but a prince of the people, destined to rule over them in the distant future.

The rest of the crown-shaped subtlety was doled out to the celebrants. Richard glanced up at the window set high in the wall above the tapestries. The sky was black; a star twinkled. The hour was late. Even for a newly made prince of Wales. Especially when he was just a little boy.

It was time for the feasting to end. Richard glanced at Anne and inclined his chin slightly, signalling wordlessly his wish to leave the festivities. Together, the king and queen rose in their heavy, jewelled robes, and the chatter in the hall ceased. Walking in stately fashion, they exited the banqueting hall, taking young Edward with them, their departure accompanied by the fanfare of trumpets.

Servants carrying lanterns led the way to the guest apartments of the bishop's palace. The first chamber was that allotted to Edward's nurses and attendants. The boy was ushered within, but even as Anne was escorted away to her room by her ladies-in-waiting, the king motioned that he would not seek his own lodgings just yet, but enter his son's chamber. He watched as the nursemaids made Edward ready for bed. When they were done, he gestured them away and lifted Edward himself, much to the attendant's surprise, to place the child in the tall, oak-framed bed and draw the coverlets over him.

'I do not know if I can sleep, Lord Father,' Edward whispered. 'It is odd not being in the nursery at Middleham.'

'I know,' said Richard. 'But you have nought to fear here in York where our family is much loved. And you must rest. Your mother and I are proud of how you held yourself today at your investiture, but it will be all for nothing if you are unwell. Dame Idley,' he nodded towards the old woman, who had served the house of York for decades, 'would you say the prince is feverish? I do not like the redness of his cheeks.'

Anne Idley stiffly approached the bed, her keen eyes observing Edward.

'It is something he often suffers from, Your Grace. The physic is not certain why. I am sure he will outgrow it.' The governess's voice faltered, and Richard glanced sharply at her. 'I will ensure he has some of his medicine, Highness.'

Richard nodded. 'Yes. And make sure he has tincture to help him sleep. He must recover from the strain of these past few days. He is not just my greatest treasure.

He is now the treasure of the entire realm.'

'Your Grace.' Anne Idley curtseyed, and the king left the room.

He paused in the corridor. He was not ready to retire yet. He had to speak with someone ... if he could find him. He had spotted the man amongst the feasters but had not spoken to him since he sent him on his mission.

James Tyrell, who had ridden to London in great haste to obtain clothes from the wardrobe for Richard's triumphant entrance into York. Tyrell, who went on other business besides.

The king saw Francis Lovell ahead of him, preparing to seek his own lodgings for the night.

'Francis, my friend,' he said warmly, striding in his direction. 'Could you do something for me?'

'Of course, my liege ... Richard,' said Francis. 'I am ever at your service.'

'Find James Tyrell. I have not managed to speak to him since he brought the royal garments from London. I wish for him to meet with me alone. In the garden.'

If Francis was perturbed by his king's request, his face did not show it.

'I spoke to him earlier, Your Grace. I will send him to you as soon as possible.'

'Thank you, my friend,' said Richard, warmly, clapping him on the shoulder. But there was a trace of weariness in his voice, and the flickering cressets in the hall sent shadows snaking down his cheeks, making them appear hollow and drawn.

He turned and made his way swiftly back down the corridor, while Francis hurried off in pursuit of James Tyrell. And the king was thinking not of Edward, his son, but of another child. No, two children.

Two boys he had left in the Tower of London.

*

The garden was cool, bathed in a blueish light cast by a

half-moon that rode upon a palanquin of clouds, its aspect red-gold, heralding the harvest.

Beneath the king's feet, the earth gave off a damp, pungent, pleasant smell that mingled with the odour of herbs and flowers in the bishop's garden. Beyond the encircling wall, the towers of the Minster reached into the heavens, impaling the stars upon their spires and giving the onlooker the impression of a celestial crown.

Richard stared up, awed as he always was when he viewed that glorious and holy building. To see the stars arranged so – it was almost like an omen, a sign that his kingship was meant to be.

He turned on his heel as he heard the soft hiss of feet on the dewy, pungent grass. James Tyrell was approaching him, a tall, thin man with a serious countenance.

A trustworthy man who had served him for ten years and had joined his ducal council.

Tyrell dropped to one knee upon the damp grass, bowing his head in deference. 'Your Grace.'

'Oh, rise, rise,' said Richard, waving a hand. 'Alone, we do not need such formalities. We have known each other for many years. And I would not have you ruin your garments for a moment's courtesy that no one else will witness.'

Tyrell hastily got to his feet.

'I summoned you here to thank you,' continued Richard, 'for riding the long miles to attend to matters of import in London.'

He fell silent. James Tyrell was also silent. But something passed between the two men, brief and sharp as lightning.

'Did it all go well?' asked Richard in a soft voice. He toyed with the ring on his smallest finger, as he always did when he grew nervous. 'You went to the Tower, spoke with Brackenbury?'

'I did, my lord king,' said James.

'And you were able … to do as I bade you ere you

left my entourage?'

He nodded. 'Yes, Your Grace. I did exactly as you asked. I pray I did it well enough that it will not be discovered by those who would plot against you.'

'That is in God's hands,' said Richard distantly, as if speaking a well-worn platitude that he only half believed in. Then a spasm of worry crossed his features, and he twisted his ring again, almost driving the metal band into his flesh. 'Was ... was Henry Stafford there? Anywhere in London at all?'

'No, my lord king. He was not. If he had been, there might have been trouble. After all, he is high constable. He could have overridden Brackenbury and gained access.'

Richard took a deep, relieved breath. 'You know that we parted on ill terms in Gloucester, Buckingham and I.'

Again, James nodded. He had travelled with the king on his progress from the very start; had seen Buckingham, who had left London late for unknown reasons, gallop up to the hostelry of the abbey in Gloucester where the king was staying. A private meeting had taken place, but after a few minutes, angry shouting filled the air, making all the courtiers and nobles grow still and pale. The king's guards drew their blades, but before they could reach the room where the king and Stafford had met, Buckingham flung the door open and stormed out, his jowly face dark as a thundercloud. He had clumsily leapt astride his steed, bawling at his accompanying retinue to take horse, and the party had raced out of the town as if demons from hell were nipping their heels.

Or an angry boar ...

At the time, Richard had given few clues as to the nature of the argument. But, soon, word had come that Buckingham was back in Brecknock, and, hearing this news, the king had looked as if a weight had been lifted from his shoulders.

'Ha! I am sure Harry will come around

eventually,' he said now, though he was not looking at Tyrell – almost as though he were speaking to himself, convincing himself that the duke's anger could be quelled. 'I am sure he still wants to get his hands on the Bohun inheritance. That I can grant him, though it must go before Parliament. However,' he shook his head, the shadows returning to his eyes, 'there were things he suggested that can never be. Never. He should never have spoken such words, and he had the gall to say it was for me …'

James Tyrell stared over Richard's shoulder into the darkness. None of Richard's friends had liked the loud, arrogant Henry Stafford, but briefly, the king seemed enamoured of the man, so much so that he allowed Buckingham to usurp the time-honoured positions of others at his coronation. James gleaned an idea of what Stafford had said when Richard gave him urgent instructions that had nought to do with the raiment he was set to bring to York from the Great Wardrobe.

'I can trust your discretion, as ever, I presume?' Richard reached out and clasped Tyrell's shoulder. A surprising familiarity for a king, perhaps, but just a few months ago he had been only a duke, and one with a closely knit band of northern allies.

James glanced at Richard's visage again. The care and worry were back. A little knot of fear twisted in his own belly too. What he had done would put his whole family at risk. And not just his own kin – his entire household at Gipping Hall.

'You can always trust me, my lord king,' he said slowly. 'I will swear an oath if you wish it.'

'No,' said Richard, his smile brittle. 'You have served me long and well. I trust you. What will be, will be, will it not? Our futures are born from the vagaries of Dame Fortune and the endless turn of her wheel.'

'That is indeed so, Your Grace.'

Richard wrapped his robes around him and gazed heavenward. 'It has grown colder, and the moon is beginning to wester. I deem it time we both sought our nightly rest.'

'As you say, my liege.'

'I will bid you a goodnight then, James. And again, I thank you for your assistance in this ... *enterprise*.'

Richard walked away without glancing back, leaving James Tyrell in the cool of the archbishop's garden. The older man waited till the monarch was gone, then took a single coin from his belt-pouch and flipped it into one of the nearby fishponds. It cleaved the still surface, the reflected moon and stars breaking apart on the ripples it made.

A penny for luck. For his own and for that of King Richard, third of that name.

*

King Richard and his entourage left York later in September. While in the town, he had gathered prominent citizens to him, listening to their troubles and complaints – the poor condition of some streets, the derelict buildings, the recent decline in industry and trade.

Richard offered to reduce the fee farm due annually to the crown. 'More trade must come to York,' he said. 'So I would have it that even those from beyond its walls are permitted to lawfully trade in the market without a toll.'

This seemed to please the mayor and many others besides.

As Richard departed through Micklegate, the road thronged with spectators, his heart was sore. Would anything in his reign ever compare to these joyous days in his favourite city? But even more than that, he sorrowed, for he must soon part from little Edward, who would return to the safety of Middleham Castle. The child was well, Dame Idley's ministrations settling him once again, but he was still not strong enough to travel further south.

The king and queen's entourage travelled a little

way upon the road that led from York and then, at a crossroads, divided into two. Edward was numbered among the smaller group, along with his mother, who would accompany him to Middleham.

'I wish I could come with you, Father,' he said, poking his tousled head through the curtains of his chariot. Today, in his plain travelling garb, he no longer looked princely, just an ordinary little boy eager to set out into the world. 'To see Pontefract and Gainsborough and Lincoln.'

'There will be time for that when you are older and stronger,' Richard told him. 'Go, in peace, my most beloved son, and do right by your tutors and nurses in order to honour me and your mother, the queen.'

Edward sighed but knew it was pointless – and unprincely – to argue.

'I hope I see you soon, Lord Father,' he said. With tears in his eyes, he retreated into the chariot, and the two groups parted, going their separate ways.

Richard turned his face to the road ahead, its rutted length twisting away to a hazy horizon. His royal visit to York – so splendorous some called it a second coronation – had been a time he would always remember, and he was reluctant to leave behind such a welcome and the safety and acceptance it promised. But he recognized that even kingly guests could grow tiresome for their hosts after a while.

And expensive.

The celebration in York was over, but there would be others just as happy and memorable in the future. Wouldn't there?

He noticed Tyrell riding to his right amidst his retinue. A loyal man, like Francis and Rob Percy. A friend who had helped *remove* a large problem, though not in the way Henry Stafford had suggested. With a jolt, he realized he had not, even for one brief second, thought of Buckingham as a friend. Not anymore.

A wave of uneasiness rushed over him as he thought of the duke closeted in Brecknock Castle with the devious Bishop Morton.

But then he thrust that thought away. Now was here. His true friends were beside him, good companions for the road and for whatever the future held. He mused on the words of Cicero, written long ago about such companionship, and he smiled as the banners blew out in the wind and the entourage moved on.

'Amicus certus in re incerta cernitur.'
('A sure friend is discerned in an unsure situation.')

About the author

J. P. Reedman lives in Wiltshire near to Stonehenge. Born in Canada, she has had a lifelong interest in ancient and medieval history, and is often found lurking, camera in hand, around prehistoric sites, ruined castles and abbeys, and interesting churches. She became a full-time writer in 2018. Her book series include *I, Richard Plantagenet*, five books chronicling King Richard's life from childhood to Bosworth, and *Medieval Babes*, a set of standalone novels about lesser-known medieval queens and noblewomen. Her most recent release is *Princess in the Police Station*, the tale of little Anne Mowbray, wife of the younger 'Prince in the Tower', whose grave was unexpectedly found in the 1960s. The next book to be released will be *The Melancholy of Winter*, about Edmund of Rutland, Richard's tragic elder brother.

Amazon:	http://author.to/ReedmanRichardII
Twitter:	https://x.com/stonehenge2500
Facebook:	https://www.facebook.com/IRichardPlantagenet
Tiktok:	https://www.tiktok.com/@janetreedman8

Watchers

Alex Marchant

We are battle-watchers, my sisters, brothers and me. We soar upon the breeze. We wait, we watch.

The grey crow, the mist crow, the gore crow.

We watch. We wait.

While armies of men close upon each other far below, clash, push one way, shove back another. Eddies in the sea. Waves upon the shoreline.

The battle cries, the shouts, the clang of arms, of shields. The screams, the groans.

The sharp scent of blood drifts upon the battle wind. The tang of fear, of despair.

We are battle-watchers, flesh-tearers, carrion-stealers.

Circling high above the battle plain. Or perched upon a tree, a rock, humped, hunched. We wait, we watch.

Until it ends…

Then we glide, we swoop, we keen, dive.

Seekers of corpses, renders of bodies. The *caróg liath*, the dolmen crow. We rip sinews, tendons. Lust after flesh, blood, bone.

We are crushers of hope.

Yet before we feast, we are witnesses only.

Until…

Once – when the mother of the mother of my mother whirled on high. She scented, saw, the great warrior, Cuchulain, hero of Ulster. Slumped, strapped, back against the pillar-stone – his defence of his countrymen at an end.

Saw his enemies all around. Hesitating, afraid. Inching closer, edging back. Waiting. Watching. Sunlight flashing on their spears, glancing off his sword.

Was he closer to death than to life?

His sword dripped blood, his side dripped blood.

The mother of the mother of my mother wheeled, she swooped. Too soon, before the battle's end, she came to rest upon his shoulder. Perched there, an executioner waiting, watching. Black hood above grey robes, black eye glinting, black beak poised. His eyes empty. She raised her beak to strike.

His enemies knew then he was dead. That they were safe now from his sword, his spears, his victories. And craven as they were, they could cut his lifeless body from the stone where it rested – upright, defiant, as though blood still coursed fierce through his hero's veins. And they could defile him, humiliate, smite his head from his neck.

The mother of the mother of my mother: betrayer of Cuchulain. Reviled now by all the men of Ulster, she flew far from her land, shunned, exiled – banished for long centuries.

We are watchers of battles, eaters of carrion, death-seekers.

I am the hooded crow.

The ancient scent of battle drew me to this man. The stink of emotion, raw still. The grief, the shame, the guilt. His lust – for another's death, for his revenge.

I perched upon the high tower, there in the centre of the city, and watched, and waited. As he watched – watched from the dark shadows of the carved-stone doorway. Watched as the procession wound away, through the city streets, through the deafening cheers and shouts and blare of fanfares, the echoing peals of bells. As men, women, children lined the way, to greet their new young king. Tall, proud, smiling, shining. Sunlight glancing off his coronet as he strode among them.

But the man hung back, in the shadows. Watching, waiting. One hand upon his sword hilt, the other on the jewelled cross hung from a chain about his neck.

And I watched too. Eyes only for him. As my talons gripped the huge cliff of rock, fashioned by men's hands for the god they worship. Not our god or goddess – far younger than they. Brought to this island of Ireland scarce centuries ago – after the defeat and death of the great one, the great warrior of Ulster. After the shame of the mother of the mother of my mother.

We are watchers of battles, watchers for battles. We know they will come. Be it hours, days, weeks. The stench of death, of fear, of blood lust. It lures us on the wind of battle, calls to us. And we answer. Always we answer.

I followed this man as days later he took ship. As his young king, Edward, paced before him, raised his arms to the adoring, tumultuous crowds. As soldiers, warriors, clashed their weapons, as trumpets blasted, as banners fluttered. A brilliant golden sun, a white rose bright against the blue of the sky, the blue of the sea.

I soared above the many ships as they set sail, fresh breeze under my wings, dark shadow far beneath me, distant upon the planking of the decks. Salt air settling in my nostrils.

Then bright day descended to dark night, and flames blossomed in braziers upon the decks. The spit of meat roasting. The clink of jugs on cups. Sailors, soldiers, crowding round. My claws clung to wood, gripped hard the smooth spar. Yet I did not roost as the ships rode the waves into distant darkness. I listened, I heard.

Heard the voices rising towards me. The words of warriors gathered round the fires.

Speaking of the man I followed, telling his history.

'He's never made his peace with it,' said one. 'Not Lord Lovell.'

'They were friends for years, King Richard and he,' offered another.

'Since children, they say. He'll never forgive himself.'

'The old king?' A third. A boy only. Eyes wide at

the tales he heard. 'He who was killed by Tudor?'

'Aye, old King Richard,' the second man agreed. 'The third of that name in England. He who was murdered by treachery on the field of battle.'

'Lord Lovell fought beside him but could not save him.' The first again. 'When King Richard led that last charge against the Welshman, when the traitor William Stanley threw in his forces to attack the king's rear – my lord Lovell was swept away by the tide of battle while his old friend was cut down.'

'He'll never forgive himself for surviving, though to have lingered on the battlefield would have been self-slaughter – a mortal sin. Now he's just set for revenge.'

''Tis no Christian path perhaps. But he licked his wounds in sanctuary at the abbey while Tudor had himself crowned. And he swore that if his chance should come, he would seize his revenge.'

'Aye, 'tis true. And the Welsh usurper quakes in his boots at word of every rising, every revolt. And lashes out with executions and fines. This, may God help us, will be the largest and the last.'

'And if God wills it, soon my lord will watch his great friend's nephew crowned again – this time in Westminster, not Dublin, and king of all England.'

The men clustered there all nodded, old hands and newcomers alike, and raised their cups in salute and drank again to their lord. And to their king.

I waited and watched and listened, but heard no more about the man I followed. So I tucked my head beneath my wing and slept. Then, upon the morrow, I followed the ships again, and watched as the craft made landfall on a rocky shore, waited as all upon them stepped on to shingle, perched high in a tree as they camped upon a heath. And then took flight and soared high above as they marched – marched across the desolate sands and over the spine of this new land. Between towering crags of rock, down through valleys green, past the turrets of an empty castle, I followed. And waited and watched for what was to come.

Four long days they marched, then four more. Men came to join them, and my brethren gathered. None were quite like my sisters, my brothers. All were full death-shrouded, black as the evil deed of the mother of the mother of my mother. And many they were who circled and dived and cried harsh into the wind. Yet I kept apart, my eyes only for he who rode shrouded in grief and sorrow, shame and guilt. I watched and waited.

Then, before another day had passed, all waiting was done. Across the way mustered a second army, larger still than this first. And as we rode upon the breeze, wheeling high above green, corn-waving fields, drumming began, the thunder of cannon, the clash of arms. The shouts, curses, shrieks of pain. The screaming of horses, the plaintive, pitiful mewling of men.

My cousins and I wove our dark patterns against the sky, watching, waiting, swooping, soaring. As first one army, then the other, advanced, retreated, charged, was forced back. As one king waited, watched, dragon-wrapped, from behind the lines of battle. As the other – golden sun, white rose shining – rallied his knights about him, prepared to enter the struggle. As the man I followed kissed the cross looped about his neck, hefted his lance, snapped down his visor, saluted his king.

A hundred voices were raised, drifting up on the battle wind to where we glided, watched, waited.

'A York, a York! God for Edward and England!'

Hooves pawed the ground, steel gauntlets on reins urged the horses on, and a hundred riders charged as one towards their enemy.

Yet the day would not be theirs. From my vantage high above, soaring with my cousins, I watched the ebb and flow of battle, saw this last desperate charge of the young king and his companions, heard the crash of metal and cries of men as they were swallowed up in the dragon's maw.

Felt the sharp stab first of halberd, then of sword as the man I followed was caught by the heat of the fight, breathed in the hot scent of blood gushing, tasted his despair.

All was lost.

We are battle-seekers, carrion-tearers, death-watchers. We do not interfere in the affairs of men. Save once. When the great hero fell. And now once more...

I swoop, I dive. I drive his horse – mad now with fear of me – from the sea of carnage. The man clutches, unseeing, at reins, at mane, at bleeding side – unable to stop the gallop, unable to stem the flow. Weak now, fingers barely grasping his sword, slumping over the neck of his terrified mount as I follow him away from the battlefield.

Down hill, past trees, across river, through fields. Away from the sigh of dying battle, the cries of my cousins as they settle now upon their prey.

At last the horse slows, driven no more by grey wings, black beak, black eye, as I watch, wait, again on high.

The man tumbles to earth, little strength left. Crawls to a nearby gatepost, drags himself upright to face what will come, grips his blade as best he can. Mutters prayers to the mother of his god. Fingers creep to the jewel upon his breast.

Pursuers are on their way. He hears the pounding hooves, the triumphant shouts, sees pointing hands, soldiers dismounting, hefting spears. Feels them pause as they see him facing them, sword in hand.

Memories of the mother of the mother of my mother course through me. Thoughts of her guilt, her grief, her shame. Of the hero she betrayed to his enemies. Of the dishonour he suffered at their hands. Of her long exile, abhorred by men.

Mingled too are nearer thoughts. This man's thoughts. Of his friend butchered by traitors on a battlefield. Stripped and paraded through streets for all to gawp at. Displayed three days on a church floor. A hasty, unmarked burial. Humiliated, defiled. And now, today, the slaughter of another young king…

His hand tightens on his sword hilt. Fingers tighten on the cross.

Do his prayers reach his god? Does mother speak to mother? Goddess perhaps to goddess…

I know not. But dishonour, guilt, shame circle down through centuries.

Spare him this… Spare us…

Beside me now, another appears. Grey, black, soaring, gliding.

I wait and watch no longer. As his enemies hesitate, uncertain, as he leans there against the pillar-stone, as they watch for him to move … Is he closer to death than to life?

We swoop, we dive. So quick, we are shadows only to all who see.

We come to rest upon his shoulders. Turn our black eyes to him. To them.

Their eyes widen.

And, beneath our claws, he shivers into dust.

Author's note

Watchers *was written specially for inclusion in* Clamour and Mischief, *an anthology of short stories about the corvids – crows and their cousins – edited by Narrelle Harris and published by Clan Destine Press (2022). Covering similar ground to my* Sons of York, *it follows Viscount Francis Lovell, who, as readers of this anthology are perhaps more likely to know, was friend and chamberlain of Richard III. Two years after the battle of Bosworth, he was a leader in a major rebellion in favour of a young king crowned in Christ Church Cathedral, Dublin. After the landing of a small army in 'Lancashire over the Sands' and a swift march across the Pennine Hills to Richard's Yorkshire heartland, this rebellion reached its climax at the battle of Stoke in June 1487. The defeat of the Yorkist army confirmed the reign of the new Lancastrian king, Henry Tudor, who famously took no direct part in either battle.*

The identity of the young Dublin King is still hotly debated. Officially recorded by Tudor chroniclers as an imposter named 'Lambert Simnel', he is documented by others as a nephew of Richard III, possibly the young King Edward V. Edward was set aside before Richard ascended the throne in 1483, having been proclaimed illegitimate owing to the bigamy of his father, King Edward IV. Francis Lovell's fate at or after the battle of Stoke remains unknown.

One Night in Coldridge

Alice Mitchell

30th November 1499

The deer are still rutting. One last melancholic bellow comes from the leftover, the forgotten and unsuccessful stag. It is late November, with the keenness of an early frost in the air, and I sup my ale by the fire, listening to his aggression, roaring like a rival king, as I press a cloth to my poor mouth to catch the drips.

I am sore at heart, knowing now what happened seven days ago in London. My little brother Richard, duke of York, his handsome face beaten to a pulp, was executed by the usurper Henry Tudor, hung like a common criminal at Tyburn, cut down and beheaded afterwards with his head spiked on London Bridge for the crows and all to see. Our cousin Edward, son of the duke of Clarence, was beheaded too at Tower Hill, that simple young man who 'couldn't tell a goose from a capon' and who never did and never would do anyone harm. But it is Richard I grieve most for. He was always livelier, more comely and more charming than I, with boundless confidence.

Yet I was once passing handsome too. Now my left eye is almost closed and the great gashing scar across my cheek and mouth draws back my lips like a snarling animal. It still aches and feels tight. Children stare and some recoil in fear. Not a good look for a king. Neither is my speech commanding, for I slur and stumble over thickened words and have much ado in the effort to get them out. This was my lot in return for a safe passage from Stoke Field and has guaranteed my anonymity here. There was no other choice. And, after all, if they said what they did about my Uncle Richard when they discovered his back was misshapen – making him out to be a hunchback and a cripple, and evil because of it, none of which was true – what would they say about me – not limping but leering, with my constant drool?

I ought to write all this down, but I know I won't.

I was certainly more confident once. When my father, King Edward IV, was alive and I was prince of Wales. I did not expect him to die so young. No one did. Nor to be king myself aged just twelve. Except that is not how it turned out, for I was never crowned, at least not in England. I had been brought up in Ludlow Castle, as was the custom for the Yorkist princes of Wales, under the care of my uncle, Anthony Woodville, Earl Rivers. He set out with me and a large army for London when the news of my father's death reached us. But we were apprehended by my Uncle Gloucester at Stony Stratford, where Anthony was arrested on charges of plotting treachery to ensure his Woodville family kept control of me instead of Richard. I didn't understand the ramifications then, but now I think it was likely true, as my mother's family were greedy and grasping and ambitious, to my shame. But I was sorry to see Anthony taken away, knowing he would be almost bound to forfeit his life. My father had chosen his own brother, Richard of Gloucester, to be Protector and I knew I must trust his judgement. Not that I, as a boy, really knew my uncle, but he seemed kindly enough and was deferential towards me, pledging his loyalty without reserve.

I was conveyed, first, to the bishop of London's palace and then to the royal apartments in the Tower of London. There my brother Richard was allowed to join me to await my coronation, though my mother, who panicked at news of Anthony's arrest, had previously sought sanctuary in Westminster Abbey with my brother and all our sisters. Yes, my mother knew only too well the real state of affairs.

Then came the most stunning revelation. Bishop

Stillington, silenced so long by fear, came forward to declare he had performed a pre-contract of marriage between my father and another noble lady before he wed my mother. So my parents' marriage was bigamous and myself illegitimate, and everyone knows that bastards cannot ascend the throne. My father had attainted the son of Clarence previously for his father's treason, and so the Lords Spiritual and Temporal and Parliament petitioned Uncle Richard to be king as the next legal and legitimate heir. I remember my tremendous disappointment at the time. But now I think maybe it was for the best, for my uncle had more experience and wisdom than a mere twelve-year-old boy. So, what became of me? Well, I was obviously not murdered in the Tower on my uncle's orders, as so many later said.

I ought to write all this down, but I can't.

For a while I remained in the Tower, though the number of my servants was reduced. But I still had my tutor and doctor and little seemed to have changed. My days were enlivened by the company of my brother, who was just nine years old then. He loved dancing and music and playing on the clavichord, which fell deafly on my ears, but we also practised archery together. That was a good time. I hadn't known Richard much before as he was brought up chiefly at court, but I got to know him then and found him a delight. He was constantly chattering and trying to cheer me up. For I was often afflicted with a sense of anxiety and foreboding. This was not misplaced, for in July of that year several men were arrested for planning to abduct us. God knows what for, but there were rumours of uprisings against the king, so we might be used as pawns. John Howard, the duke of Norfolk, was sent to secure our safety. Clearly we had to be moved, and it was thought better to separate us, so we were parted once more. Howard arranged for Richard to go to Europe, and I never saw him again till two years ago. I was taken to a multitude of places, but eventually ended up here in Coldridge, deep in Devonshire.

Then the Wheel of Fortune turned again, as it is wont to do. Henry Tudor invaded and Uncle Richard was killed in battle at Bosworth field, fighting bravely but betrayed. Tudor became king by conquest alone and married my sister Elizabeth to shore up his tenuous claim to the throne. To do this he had to remove the bastardy on us all, overturning King Richard's Act of Titulus Regius which he tried to destroy. In which case, it would appear I am the rightful king after all. Henry had no idea where I was, but issued a proclamation begging me to come forward if I was still alive to make my claim. I wasn't fool enough to fall for that, to end up in captivity or worse. But then my Aunt Margaret, dowager duchess of Burgundy, and her son-in-law King Maximilian took much time and trouble and spent a great deal of monies to equip me with two armies to invade England and be restored to the throne. Even my mother pledged her support, and so did my cousin John de la Pole, earl of Lincoln, who had been heir-apparent to King Richard before.

So I was taken to Dublin and crowned in the cathedral there, being sixteen now and deemed to have attained my majority. What a heady time that was! The Irish lords were jubilant. They had to borrow the crown from a statue of the Virgin Mary, but afterwards I was borne in triumph through streets of cheering crowds on the broad shoulders of the great William Darcy.

I really should write all this down, but I shan't.

In 1487 we invaded England with the first army, but it all ended calamitously at the battle of Stoke Field. I did not have to fight myself but sat astride my horse, watching from what we thought was a safe distance. I was horrified and appalled. There was so much carnage, such bloodshed and brutality and it came on me then what my Uncle Richard had to do and how he must have suffered. Watching the orange-clothed Irish kerns was the worst. They were poorly equipped and skewered with willow staves like inconsequential meat. Yet even the German mercenaries did not escape harm, with halberds and axes finding the gaps in their armour. My cousin John laid down his life for me, as did so many others. And for what? The second army never came, having been diverted to Brittany.

I was taken by Tudor's men. They spared my life but slashed my face deliberately and cruelly to disfigure me. The pain was excruciating. Then they substituted another lad for me, calling him an imposter named Lambert Simnel, and took him away, putting him to work in the royal kitchens to humiliate him. Only the Irish lords were not deceived. He was younger than me anyway, so the ruse was laughable.

I was taken away from the field by a small party of Tudor's men, but somehow a group of loyal Yorkist survivors managed to overcome them on their way and secure my escape. And so I returned here to Coldridge. I heard my mother was sent to Bermondsey Abbey to live out the rest of her days in poverty. She will not have liked that.

But I am better by far here, away from Westminster. It is a relief to me to pursue a quiet life of reading and contemplation, with my dogs and horses and the deer. I may ride freely over the gorse-strewn moors nearby, with the sea-blown wind in my hair, and I have a few trusted companions who will not betray me. Like a leprechaun cobbling shoes, I keep misery and boredom at bay with my work as the parker and overseeing the flour mill.

Only my little brother could not let things rest. I did not object to him taking over my claim to the throne. I had tried and failed, and am no longer regal or prepossessing in my appearance. But I feared for Richard. He came to visit me on his way to Exeter with his fighting men two years ago. So bright, so confident. So determined – at first – not to be called an imposter. Later stepping out proudly in cloth of gold to face his captivity when his uprising inevitably failed. Until they tortured him to extract a confession and called him Perkin Warbeck. They kept him at court for nigh on two years and made his wife my sister Elizabeth's lady in waiting. Elizabeth must have known the truth, and I wonder if she feels as sore at heart as I do now.

The woodsmoke comforts me as the fire burns low and the candles flicker. Richard is gone, just as the last rutting deer will be soon. The hot bloody smell of venison – ripe for the taking – seems to assail my nostrils. The very last bellow – a roar of impotent rage – rings out from beyond the pale.

I am no longer a boy, nor even a young man, and certainly not a king. I am John Evans, the parker of Coldridge Manor farms. It will be winter soon, and I shall enter my thirties next year. My father died when he was barely forty. Perhaps my thoughts should turn to building a chantry chapel in the church here. For this is my home and I am not short of money. I shall indeed make a pledge to do so.

I ought to write all this down, but I know I won't.

Edward and Richard Plantagenet are no more, and any son of mine shall not bear that name. The Yorkist hopes are gone forever. The stags are dead after one last howl.

About the author

Alice Mitchell is the pen name of Dr Alison Harrop who is a member of the committee of the Yorkshire branch of the Ricard III Society and editor of the branch magazine, *Blanc Sanglier*. Also a novelist, she is author of *The Mortimer Affair: Joan de Joinville's Story*, which covers the events of the turbulent reign of Edward II from the perspective of Lady Joan Mortimer, wife of the infamous Roger Mortimer and an ancestor of Ricard III. Her latest book, *The Golden Door* (Arcanum, 2024), concerns a diverse group of mid-nineteenth-century emigrants to America.

Website: www.alicemitchell.co.uk

A Winter's Tale

Darren Harris

In the chill winter air, six stone grotesques stared down from the parapet of Leicester Cathedral: a fox, tiger, wyvern, peregrine falcon, and a Longwool sheep, five animals associated with the city, and a white boar, symbol of the king buried within the cathedral itself. Beneath them, under the sharp white stare of streetlights, lazily drifting snowflakes began to settle, forming a thin, opaque blanket around the cathedral. A young couple laden with bags of Christmas shopping scurried past the ancient holy building, squelching the wet snow underfoot as they made their way to catch a bus home.

A cat, black as the depths of night save for two yellow eyes, ran past the wooden beams and limewashed walls of the medieval Guildhall, then disappeared between the iron railings of a gate opposite the cathedral. Somewhere nearby a clock struck six and, as if taking the chimes as its cue, the snow fell faster, in large, crisp white flakes, swirling rhythmically, before landing, layer upon layer, covering the ice-mush footprints the Christmas shoppers left behind.

Despite its size, the open space inside the cathedral was warm, thanks in part to the heated limestone floor, recently installed. Having worked in many a draughty church, Reverend Thomas appreciated the warmth and the work put in to renovating the old building. She cast her gaze up to the ceiling running from the sanctuary to the east window. The spaces between the roof boards were painted midnight blue, giving the impression of the heavens opening out above the onlooker. She wondered how many visitors realized the scattering of tiny stars adorning this heavenly canvas were not actually stars but cinquefoils, five-leaf flowers from the city of Leicester's coat of arms. She looked around the cathedral, admiring the work done to bring it into the twenty-first century – to make it a modern civic space and place of worship, and a fitting resting place for King Richard III.

Revd Thomas picked up a tablet and pressed the screen to adjust the spotlights and pendent lighting above. Now all the visitors had left, there was no need to highlight every nook and cranny. She preferred a more ambient level of lighting that was easier on the eyes. As she placed the tablet back on a table, something at the far end of the cathedral caught her eye. She peered at the space between two pillars where she thought she had seen movement. No one should be in the cathedral now; all the visitors had gone, and she had locked the door behind the last of the volunteers to leave the building. Perhaps she had just imagined it. Or maybe it was one of the pennants in the ambulatory around King Richard's tomb. Except … there was no breeze inside the cathedral to move it. Revd Thomas turned to look at the Royal Leicestershire regimental flags hanging in St George's chapel to prove to herself she was right. The flags hung limp and lifeless, and she felt her stomach tighten with a sense of unease.

This is nonsense, she thought. She wasn't sure what she had seen, or if indeed she had seen anything, but she steeled herself to go and find out. She took a deep breath and exhaled sharply before walking along the south aisle, past the medieval chapel, towards where she had spied the movement. She rounded the corner of St Dunstan's chapel and entered the chancel where King Richard lay at rest. There she was greeted by a most extraordinary sight.

A strange-looking gentleman stood at the foot of the king's tomb with his head bowed and his hands clasped tight in front of him. His hairline had receded so the top of his head was completely bald, yet his hair was long at the back and sides. The dark locks were frizzy and bushed out behind, in stark contrast to his spindly, copper-brown moustache which failed to join his straggly, pointed beard. He wore a gold hooped earring as though unable to let go of a misspent youth. But strangest of all was his attire.

An odd-shaped jacket of dark green cloth, fastened with a row of closely spaced buttons, drew in at the waist, then came to a point below. It was decorated with silver thread down the front and around the shoulders, which overhung the sleeves, making the shoulders appear broader than they really were. A white linen shirt peeked out, folded back over at the collar and cuffs. Completing the outfit were baggy shorts of the same material as the jacket, worn over grey woollen leggings, and brown leather shoes with rough hand-stitched seams. The man looked like a child's drawing of a pirate. Revd Thomas guessed he was a historical re-enactor, probably taking part in an event at the Guildhall next door.

'I'm sorry, but the cathedral is closed,' she informed him.

'Do you suppose he's happy?' the man asked, still staring at King Richard's tomb.

'Er, I suppose so,' the Reverend said, caught off-guard by the question. 'But we're closed. The cathedral closed to visitors at six.'

The man turned his head towards her and smiled. A warm, kind smile beneath eyes of deep chocolate brown.

'Just a moment more of your time, please, dear lady.'

He spoke quietly, calmly. But Revd Thomas sensed something in his voice. The man was in need. She couldn't tell why, or in need of what. It was just a feeling, but she knew he wanted to stay and talk. She couldn't deny a person in need.

'I have a few moments before I prepare for the evening service,' she said.

The man turned back to face the tomb.

'It is a simple yet interesting monument,' he

declared. 'Not how I imagined the tomb of a medieval king.'

'He was reburied in the twenty-first century, so his tomb reflects that part of his journey,' the Reverend said. 'It's made from Swaledale limestone, quarried in North Yorkshire. Yorkshire stone for a Yorkist king. Fitting, don't you think?'

The man just shrugged, so Revd Thomas tried to lighten the mood.

'It's polished to a fine finish so you can see all the long-dead creatures immortalized in the stone. There's even a fossilized shark's tooth here.' She crouched to point at a dark spot on the side of the tombstone.

But the man continued staring at the cross marking King Richard's tomb.

'The deep-cut cross symbolizes King Richard's piety and his deeply held Christian belief,' the Reverend explained. 'If you stand at the foot of the cross and look along its length, you'll see it's been carved in such a way that the shadow within comes to a point so it looks like a sword. A Christian cross and a warrior's sword to represent two sides of a medieval king.'

'Two sides of a medieval king?' the man mused, tugging at his lower lip. 'Tell me more of King Richard.'

'Well, his remains lie in a lead ossuary which is itself in a coffin made from English oak. The coffin was placed in a brick-lined vault below the...'

'No, not his burial. Tell me of the man himself,' the man demanded. 'His character, his deeds. An honest tale speeds best, being plainly told.'

What an odd way of putting it, thought the Reverend. *He's certainly immersed in his work as a historical re-enactor.* She chuckled inwardly, then asked, 'Does this period of history particularly interest you?'

'All periods of history interest me,' the man replied. 'But I fear I have misunderstood this man and his deeds. Much of what I know comes from the writings of Thomas More and Raphael Holinshed. Methinks they may have painted a portrait of Richard of Gloucester's character with brushes as crooked as his own hunched back.'

'King Richard had scoliosis, yes, but he wasn't a hunchback,' the Reverend said.

The man looked confused.

'I, that am curtailed of this fair proportion, Cheated of feature by dissembling nature. Deformed, unfinished, sent before my time, into this breathing world, scarce half made up,' he quoted.

Ah, he's not a historical re-enactor, he's a Shakespearean actor.' And suddenly it made sense to Revd Thomas. Perhaps this man thought Shakespeare's plays were historical facts.

'That's just Tudor propaganda,' she said. 'King Richard had scoliosis, a curvature of the spine, and probably would have had one shoulder higher than the other. But he definitely wasn't a hunchback. He was well able to ride a horse and fight. In fact, he was acclaimed in his own time as an accomplished warrior. He led a wing of King Edward's army into battle at Barnet and Tewkesbury, as well as his infamous cavalry charge at Bosworth. Now that's hardly something you'd expect a hunchback to be doing, is it?

'In fact,' she continued, 'according to John Rous, the Tudor historian, King Richard "bore himself like a gallant knight and acted with distinction as his own champion until his last breath." And the Crowland Chronicle describes him falling on the battlefield, struck by many mortal wounds, as a bold and most valiant prince.'

'True, he was a famed and valiant warrior,' the man conceded, then recited, 'And thus I clothe my naked villainy, with old odd ends stolen out of holy writ; And seem a saint, when most I play the devil.'

'Oh, don't get me wrong,' Revd Thomas countered. 'Like any medieval king, he was probably no angel. But was he as black as history has painted him?'

'The prince of darkness is a gentleman!'

'No, I'm not saying that either. But was he really as bad as you seem to think he was?'

'I am determined to prove a villain, and hate the idle pleasures of these days. Plots have I laid, inductions dangerous...'

'You're quoting the Bard again, aren't you?' the Reverend interrupted. 'Well, I do think King Richard has been painted as a bad character over the years, whereas he actually did much good in his lifetime.'

'Ha!' the man scoffed. 'Pray, do tell me of these so-called good deeds.'

'King Richard was a social and legal reformer,' the Reverend explained, undeterred. 'He reformed the system of bail to ensure it was freely available to everybody, whether they could afford justice or not, and therefore ended the practice of indefinite imprisonment of those accused of a crime, whether innocent or guilty. A good thing, don't you think?'

The man stood, arms folded across his chest, staring at the limestone tomb without uttering a word in reply.

He's a tough nut to crack, the Reverend thought.

'King Richard also ended the practice of seizing the personal property of people held on suspicion of committing a crime,' she carried on. 'Before this, their goods could be forfeited as soon as they were accused, and even if they were later proved innocent, there was no requirement for their property to be returned. He also made it more likely that people would receive a fair trial in sheriff's courts by only allowing people worth more than twenty shillings a year to serve on juries.'

The man's interest was piqued. 'And how would this make a fair trial more likely?'

'It was generally believed that if a person was well off, they would be less susceptible to bribery.'

'I suppose that makes sense,' the man said.

'But that's not all. Richard's first act as king was

to instruct judges to issue justice without regard to a person's wealth, power or position in society. He also instigated the Court of Requests, which allowed the poor, for the very first time, access to legal advice regardless of their financial means. This applied to many people, particularly women. The lawyers of the common law courts lost business because of it, but King Richard never shied away from upsetting the rich and powerful if it resulted in fairness and equity for the poorer or least represented members of society.'

'I didn't know any of that,' the man confessed. 'You seem to know a great deal about King Richard.'

'When you have a king of England buried in your cathedral, it's important to know about him. Did you know he created land rights too, so a person could no longer sell land and conceal that a part of the property had already been sold to someone else? And he abolished the monarch's absolute right to seize the lands and bodies of child heirs. His parliament also passed an Act standardizing measurements so people knew how much they were getting for their money and were protected from dishonest dealers.'

The man smiled at that.

The Reverend was in full flow now.

'Another Act prohibited the import of many small manufactured goods, which protected English traders. But one proviso Richard himself may have added to the Act was that no restrictions were imposed on imports of written or printed books. King Richard understood the importance of education and collected books himself, so he knew the benefits of fostering printing and encouraging learning through books. When he became king, he also ordered that new laws be written in English rather than in Latin and French, and displayed in public areas, so that ordinary people could see and understand them. You can't disagree that King Richard did much good and that many who benefited from his policies were ordinary folk, the poor, the unrepresented, and the powerless.'

The man gave an almost imperceptible nod.

'All this in a reign of just two years,' the Reverend enthused. 'Imagine what he could have done if he'd reigned for longer!'

'This is interesting,' the man admitted. 'He passed many good laws. But what of him as a man rather than as a lawgiver? Do you know of any good deeds that he did personally?'

'I think his acts as king show what he was like as a man,' said the Reverend. 'But, yes, there are examples of him personally helping people. Take the case of Katherine Bassingbourne of York, whose father's will stated his house should pass to his widow, Ellyn, then to Katherine and her heirs. Ellyn remarried and when she died, Katherine's stepfather tried to claim the property. When Katherine appealed to Richard for help, he personally intervened to ensure Katherine's case was heard and that she was treated fairly.'

'Yes, yes,' the man said dismissively, 'but that is Richard in his capacity as king and lawgiver. What of him personally helping others before he was king?

'Well, a decade before that, Richard took a father and three sons into his service. He soon discovered the sons were accused of murdering a man, and they'd all entered Richard's service for protection. Noblemen usually protected those in their service, even if they knew they'd done wrong. But Richard arrested the father and, when the sons fled, put out a warrant for their arrest. Rather than protect his own retainers, Richard chose to support a widow seeking justice for her murdered husband. There are numerous other examples of Richard helping others. Even one occasion that could have brought Richard into conflict with his own mother.'

'Pray tell,' the man said, clearly intrigued.

'A couple were forced to flee their manor when attacked by a wealthy goldsmith and his men,' the Reverend explained. 'When the attackers occupied the manor, the sheriff issued a warrant against them. The goldsmith was in Richard's service and argued that Richard would protect him. But the husband and wife were in the service of Richard's mother, Cecily. Richard convened a panel of lawyers to investigate, with half provided by himself and half by his mother. The lawyers found in the couple's favour and the property was returned to them. But Richard didn't leave the matter there. The goldsmith had to appear before the King's Council and he was told never to bring Richard's name into disrepute again.'

Revd Thomas's enthusiasm for defending King Richard was evident.

'Richard was also known to support the mentally ill. While he was Lord Protector, lands and possessions inherited by the Bartlett sisters were given to the crown because they were deemed not in possession of their mental faculties. Richard ordered the inheritance to be used to support the sisters for the rest of their lives. It's no wonder the Bishop of St David's said of Richard, "He contents the people wherever he goes better than ever did any prince, for many a poor man that has suffered wrong many days has been relieved and helped by him … God hath sent him to us for the welfare of us all."'

'I can see you believe King Richard to have been a benevolent man,' the man said. 'But what of the shadow cast by him? It is long, dark, and evil, for he also committed the most heinous crimes. Regardless of his good deeds, Richard of Gloucester is a murderer many times over.'

'Nonsense!' Revd Thomas declared.

'Sword, hold thy temper, heart be wrathful still. Priests pray for enemies, but princes kill,' the man retorted. 'It is known that Richard murdered the Duke of Somerset.'

'When did he do that?'

'At the first battle of St Albans. Richard hacked him down at the Castle Inn.'

'Firstly,' responded the Reverend, 'killing someone in battle isn't murder, is it? But more importantly, that battle was fought in 1455. Richard was born in 1452. Are you telling me a two- or three-year-old boy killed a grown man?'

Seeing that argument shot down in flames, the man quickly changed tack.

'But Richard did kill Prince Edward of Lancaster and King Henry VI.'

'Prince Edward died at the battle of Tewkesbury,' insisted Revd Thomas. 'And even if he survived the battle and was among those executed afterwards, it was on the orders of the king, Edward IV. The same for Henry VI. Edward had just regained the throne, having been deposed by an army acting in Henry's name. He couldn't let it happen again, so he ordered Henry's murder.'

Having put that record straight, she carried on determinedly. 'And before you accuse Richard of having a hand in his other brother's death, I can tell you George of Clarence was arrested for treason. He was tried in parliament by Edward IV himself and sentenced to death. Richard had nothing to do with it.'

The man stroked his chin, teasing his beard into a point as he stared glassy-eyed into the past.

'But, alas, dear lady,' he said, after a moment's thought, 'the die is cast and History's verdict is written. King Richard is a child killer, who murdered his nephews so he could seize the throne.'

'History can be rewritten,' the Reverend said vociferously. 'Facts can dismantle the tangled web of misinformation and propaganda that surrounds King Richard and the princes in the Tower. New facts and information are being brought to light all the time. Let me tell you, based on what we already know, why it's highly unlikely that King Richard murdered his nephews.'

'Please do, dear lady, please do.'

'Firstly, there's absolutely no evidence Richard III murdered the boys. All the so-called evidence is based upon rumours, and rumours that began on the continent, not in England where you might expect them to start. Thomas More is the most usually cited source for their deaths at Richard's hands, but even he didn't directly accuse him, again just repeating what was rumoured. And his *History of King Richard III* was never completed. It was found among his possessions after his death, was finished by someone else and published more than twenty years later. There are so many historical inaccuracies and errors in the work that very few people now take it as a valid historical source – and as More wasn't a historian, perhaps he never meant it to be.

'His claim that the boys' bodies were buried "at the stair foot" in the Tower of London is used to support the theory that the bones in a marble urn in Westminster Abbey are those of the princes. But then More's later comment that they were dug up and reburied somewhere else, since forgotten, is conveniently ignored. When those bones now in the urn were discovered under a staircase, the then king's father, Charles I, had not long before been beheaded after the civil war. So Charles II used them to remind his subjects of the dangers of deposing and murdering a king. Who knows whether he genuinely believed they were the remains of the princes?'

The man tugged at his beard as he listened to the Reverend's explanation.

'I don't believe they are,' the Reverend continued, making her own position clear. 'They were found ten feet below a staircase that had been demolished, and, based on that depth, they're most probably Roman or Saxon. The site of the Tower has been in use for a long time and many human bones have been discovered there, including a child's skeleton in 1977 that was dated to the Iron Age.'

Revd Thomas could tell the man was musing over her arguments, so she added more fuel to the fire.

'Also, consider that the boys' mother, the former queen Elizabeth Woodville, gave her daughters into Richard's care in the spring of 1484. Would she have done that if she thought for one second that he had murdered her sons? And their sister, Henry VII's wife Elizabeth of York, kept a book that had belonged to Richard, respectfully signing her name under his rather than crossing through it or tearing it out altogether. Surely those closest to the princes wouldn't act in this manner if they believed Richard had them murdered. Not one of them ever accused Richard of murdering the princes, not one!'

The man's expression was pained, but the Reverend didn't let up.

'And did you know there was a precedent for the boys surviving? When Henry IV usurped the throne in 1399, the Mortimer brothers, Edmund and Roger, were considered the true heirs of King Richard II. Henry could have had them murdered as they were a threat to him, but he didn't. He had them cared for instead, and they grew up to be loyal supporters. Why couldn't Richard have done the same?'

'The evil that men do lives after them; the good is oft interred with their bones, Aye, the king's name is a tower of strength,' the man said under his breath. Then, 'Lady, I am neither black nor white, but like all people am a shade of grey. So King Richard, much maligned by myself, was perhaps himself a lighter shade than I had presupposed. I am much distressed that my work has been taken as historical fact. I thank you for taking the time to talk to me about him. It is a fitting monument,' he agreed, gazing once more upon the king's tomb.

With that he turned on his heel and strode towards the heavy wooden cathedral door, which he swung open with ease before disappearing into the night. A flurry of snow swirled in through the opening.

I'm sure I closed that door, Revd Thomas thought as she scurried to close it to keep out the cold. When she reached the door, she froze in shock.

Snow had been falling heavily and now lay several inches thick. Street lamps illuminated the area from the cathedral entrance across to the road. It was a scene of white-blanketed serenity, with not a soul in sight. But what troubled the Reverend was that no footprint disturbed that snow. The man had walked out of the cathedral across an expanse of deep fresh snow without leaving any tracks.

'Dear God!' she exclaimed in sheer wonder. She shuddered, not with cold but at the thought of what she witnessed.

Her thoughts whirled as she tried to piece things together. *A man in Shakespearean clothing, reciting lines from Shakespeare. He wanted to know more about King Richard. He referred to his work and how he had maligned the king. He had to be an actor, he had to be ...* she tried to convince herself.

But he didn't leave any footprints!

About the author

Darren Harris was born and raised in Leicester. He has a lifelong interest in history, particularly Richard III and the Wars of the Roses, and has been teaching history in mainstream and special needs schools across Leicestershire since 2001. He is a founding member of his local heritage society and gives talks to local heritage and historical societies.

Darren's first novel, *The King's Son* (Arcanum, 2022), tells the story of Richard of Eastwell, who was buried under the name Richard Plantagenet in 1550 and is considered by some to be an illegitimate son of Richard III. The book tells Richard's story leading up to Bosworth and his part in the subsequent Yorkist risings against Henry Tudor.

Books:	https://www.amazon.co.uk/stores/Darren-Harris/author/B09MG7JRDG
Twitter:	https://x.com/DHarrisAuthor

A Middleham Fantasy

Bridget M. Beauchamp

2nd October

The late afternoon sun sank behind a menacing bank of cloud, intensifying the autumn chill hanging in the air as the wind moaned around the ancient stones of Middleham Castle. The empty windows of the old fortress, enigmatic shadows of former glory, stared out across Wensleydale like eye sockets in a skull, sightless and vacant, glassless and cold. Wild thyme and mosses clung to the sills where rooks and pigeons picked at the cracks and where ledges and missing infill afforded a night-time roost high up amongst the ramparts, now outlined against a darkening sky. The last visitors had left. The castle staff, bringing in signs and locking the cabin, chattered together about the day, before padlocking the outer gate and leaving the castle to its memories and ghosts of times long gone.

I watched from the topmost tower, King Richard III's standard still snapping in the freshening breeze, the halyard pinging against the pole just above me. Feeling guilty for my trespass, I knew I would have to climb over the gate at the rear of the site to return to my car, but I was loath to leave. I had the place to myself at last, as the shadows lengthened and crept up the high walls of the keep. Somewhat eerily, though, I felt I wasn't alone. Could I hear voices from the past echoing up the stairwell? The clattering of platters and jugs from the kitchens beneath? Laughter and shouts; prayers whispering from the chapel below me. Snippets of plainsong coming and going amidst the soughing murmur of the wind, a lament so sad, so melancholy, I wanted to weep.

Feeling my way along the damp stone walls, I crept down the staircase. The darkness pressed upon me and I hurried towards the light emanating from the landing below. Was that a footstep? I shivered as a draught of cool air blew past me like the swish of silk from a noblewoman's gown. It trailed over the steps above me and vanished up the spiral void in a rustle of dry leaves.

As I emerged on to the landing, the great hall opened out below me. But what was this? It was no longer open to the skies, but enclosed under a weighty timber ceiling, lit by huge iron candelabras and tapers. Heavy tapestries adorned the walls, shimmering threads glistening in the firelight from the enormous hearth. Long trestle tables were littered with the remnants of a feast, and servant boys and girls were busy sweeping soiled rushes into a pile. They giggled and teased one another as they laboured, then scurried down to the cookhouse below, their faces flushed from the heat. On the balcony, a group of minstrels sat supping tankards of ale, eyeing pretty maids clearing the remains of the repast, an assortment of instruments resting in impotent silence at their feet. The men whistled suggestively at the girls, who returned their stares in defiance.

Feeling like an intruder, I turned to make my way down, but as I did, a striking young man emerged from where the chapel once stood and stopped to stare in my direction. He was dressed in a mulberry velvet doublet and hose with a gold-mounted cabochon brooch pinned at his shoulder, and as I took in his slim frame, fine features and shoulder-length straight hair, his blue eyes and strong chin reminded me of an image I was momentarily unable to place.

'Who are you?' he asked in a soft tenor, not quite with the depth of a fully fledged adult male but hovering somewhere between adolescence and burgeoning manhood. I could tell he was of a high social standing. He also had an aura of greatness that I felt compelled to acknowledge. I instinctively bent my knee in deference.

'Bridget, my lord,' I replied falteringly, unsure how to address this man but conscious of my status as a low-born stranger in this noble ancestral seat.

He smiled, repeating, reflectively, 'Bridget,' then asking, 'Are you Irish?'

'I was born in England my lord,' I replied. 'But my grandmother was Irish I believe.'

Just at that moment a servant approached.

'My lord of Gloucester, the earl requests your presence in the solar.' The man bowed his head respectfully, unaware, it seemed, of my presence.

The nobleman nodded and, turning to go, said to me, with a wink, 'Duty calls.'

A sudden blast of icy air blew down the passageway, and I realized I was alone again. I turned back to gaze at the great hall below, but where was the scene I had so recently witnessed? Now it was roofless once more, the floor an empty void open to the kitchen beneath. An owl flew by silently overhead, making for a niche in the wall, where once a huge weight-bearing beam had rested. Gone were the flickering tapers; now dark, empty and cold, the fireplace was just a yawning hole. Bare walls crumbled, window openings framed vacant spaces where stone mullions once held multi-paned glass in place against the elements.

I stood still for some moments, attempting to make sense of it all. What had I seen? Had I been dreaming? Had my imagination run riot and conjured up a vision I had so longed for?

Forcing myself into action, I made my way down to ground level and walked round to the statue of Richard III where earlier I had laid a white rose in honour of his birthday. I sat down upon a low wall nearby to calm my racing heart.

Had it been Richard? Had I encountered the ghost of the man who had occupied my thoughts so often since the momentous discovery of his long-lost grave? I closed my eyes, willing him to appear to me once more, to imprint his features indelibly on my brain. But to no avail. His image remained as elusive as the phantom I had imagined.

Spots of rain splashed my head and hands, so I gathered my coat around me and hurried to the modern gate out of the castle. I climbed over its bars and ran back to my car just as larger droplets fell. I sank into the driver's seat, shutting the door firmly against the wind, as the warmth of my twenty-first-century mobile sanctuary enveloped me.

Oh, Richard, was that really you? I breathed. I smiled to myself, then suddenly perceived I was tired, so very tired, as if the rigours of time travel had exhausted my reserves. I needed to sleep before my journey home. I leant my head back and slipped into unconsciousness as the deluge beat down upon the roof.

Sometime later, I awoke to silence. The squall had passed. The moon was up and the first evening star shone like a single diamond set in an indigo sky. I turned to look up at the castle ruins, now just a black silhouette merging into the gloom.

Had I been dreaming? Did I really see him? Had our eyes met across the mists of half a millennium? Had my own ghost from the future manifested itself to him, by the sheer power of my desire? Had Richard allowed me that brief glimpse of the past? His past?

No matter. Be it a dream, invocation or apparition, that vision would stay with me forever. A moment in time, so far removed, yet somehow so near, in this historic place.

A sudden bleep interrupted my thoughts, instantly propelling me back to the present. I glanced down at my mobile phone lying on the seat beside me.

Where are you? read the text message from my grandson.

Setting off from Middleham now, I typed, pressing 'send' resignedly. Opening the window and heaving a deep breath to clear my head, I reluctantly turned the key in the ignition. Much as I yearned with every fibre of my being to be back in the fifteenth century, I didn't belong there. It was time to go home, away from this place of shadows and phantasms. Back to people who needed me now. Yet deep in my subconscious would always linger that cherished fantasy, those unspoken thoughts – 'If only…'

About the author

Bridget M. Beauchamp lives in Cumbria, where she raised her family, though she grew up in Suffolk, trained as a graphic designer in Sussex and worked in London in the 1970s, before moving to the north in the early 1980s. Since her retirement, she has renewed her lifelong interest in British history, and in particular the life and times of Richard III. She is an active member of the Richard III Society and is passionate about restoring the reputation of this much-maligned king.

Bridget's first novel, *Maid of Middleham*, follows Richard's life as seen through the eyes of a young maid in service for the earl and countess of Warwick at Middleham Castle. The sequel, *Cleave to the Crown*, continues the narrative after Richard's death at Bosworth and features Francis Lovell, the battle of Stoke and the two so-called Pretenders, who Bridget is convinced were the sons of Edward IV. Both novels were written with the intention of persuading readers to see Richard as a pious family man of integrity, a brave warrior and respected statesman, rather than the well-known Shakespearean caricature. Bridget loves Britain, its history, culture, literature, nature and landscape, which she hopes is reflected in her work.

Books:	https://www.amazon.co.uk/stores/Bridget-M.-Beauchamp/author/B0B292CJT3
Facebook:	https://www.facebook.com/p/Bridget-M-Beauchamp-100075896933487/

A Spirited and Most Courageous Prince…

Jennifer C. Wilson

England, August 1485

'*God forbid that I retreat one step.*'

And he doesn't. King Richard of England, the third of that name, truly doesn't.

Not when the news of Henry Tudor gathering forces in Normandy reaches his ears, or of his landing at Milford Haven on the seventh of August.

Not when he hears of the defection of Rhys ap Thomas, his lieutenant in west Wales, the man who had stood fast against Buckingham's rebellion of 1483.

Not when hordes of Welshmen are recruited to the Tudor cause, swelling to an army of two thousand by mid-August.

Not even when that army crosses the English border and heads for Shrewsbury.

Richard had known they were coming, of course he had. What type of king would he be if he didn't monitor possible threats? So, messages are sent, summons are issued, and orders are given: the Yorkist army is to gather in Leicester.

Once there, Richard takes a room at the Boar Inn, and after bidding his men a good night, he retires to bed. There's so much in his head, but he's determined to stay focused; he cannot fail now, not when the biggest threat to his rule is just miles away. The next few days will decide everything.

As they depart Leicester on the twenty-first,

there's an incident on the bridge. It shouldn't mean anything, the clip of metal against stone, but he hears the whispers, the mutterings, despite his best efforts to shut them out, shut all of it out. He knows what Tudor is capable of, and that there are elements of his own contingent that he cannot fully trust, but he cannot afford to think of that now. He will not think of that now. He's done all he can – gathered support, issued stern notices and veiled threats as required. Now all he can do is ride out with courage, holding fast to his closest allies, and his faith.

That night, in his tent in camp, knowing what must happen the next day, Richard begins his final checks, ensuring his armour and weapons are in good order. No, more than that: in their best order. In truth, it should be the work of his squires and servants, but tonight feels important. Tonight, he wants to make sure for himself. As he pulls cloth over metal, cleaning and polishing each plate, tiny flecks of dust and soil come away, having dried into the hilt of his sword, the ties of his harness. Soil he must have carried with him for months, if not for years.

His mind wanders, remembering the battles that have led him to this moment. The victories, the defeats. The people he has lost along the way. There is peaceful soil here, as well as that of the battlefield. Foreign soil, as well as that of home. Traces of brothers, both of blood and in arms, forged through years of strife. Memories of teaching his beloved son Edward in the tiltyard, mirroring the sparring he had enjoyed (and endured) with his own brothers – brothers no longer here.

Richard wonders for a moment whether such rememberings make him morose, his mental wanderings through memories some would advise to leave buried. But tonight, they bring comfort. The spirits of friends and family he's fought alongside since his teens can bring him strength now, help him push on, to face this challenge with everything he can muster. So that is what he will do. Gather every ounce of courage he can and draw on it now.

After finishing his preparations for next day, equipment and attire set out for easy dressing, Richard glances out of his tent, watching the camp ease itself into the night. Under his banner, the sign of the boar, he seeks an early escape into sleep. He will need all his energy for the battle ahead.

As predicted, engagement is early on the twenty-second of August. It's barely even mid-morning as Richard pauses to take stock, surveying the field. The blood isn't obvious, mixed in as it is with the liveries, the standards, the gradually dulling silver, and the mud. But he knows it's there. Whether more has been spilled of his men's or Tudor's, Richard isn't sure. It likely won't be clear until the end. But the end isn't, he hopes, coming quite yet.

At that end, whenever it comes, the blood of only one man truly matters on this field – his or Tudor's. Of course, Richard wants his men to survive, to triumph. But he knows too well what is at stake here. That the winner will take all, including the life of the loser. Richard will do the best he can: fight for all he is worth, conduct his troops to gain every advantage, and pray to God that it is enough. That the loser does not end up being him. That it's Tudor's blood that spills. It's a terrible thing to wish. Doesn't feel like the prayer of a courageous man. But Richard is certain that on the other side of the field, the same prayer, in reverse, is being sent up by Tudor himself. So he prays.

In the heat of battle, with Stanley and Northumberland failing to engage, Richard sees his chance to end this quickly, on his own terms – no reliance on unreliable commanders. Spying Tudor at the back of his forces, Richard signals to his closest comrades, the ones he knows won't abandon him in this decisive move. With the Tudor banner firmly in his sights, his mind is made up.

He charges.

In body, his contingent is small, no more than thirty men whom he trusts with his life, but in spirit, they number in their hundreds. Yorkist allies from years gone by are at his side, urging him on. The spirits of Towton, of

Barnet, of Tewkesbury – they line up, weapons primed, reminding him of victories of Yorkist past, even those he couldn't fight at himself. Anne, his beloved Anne, and their beautiful son, Edward, are there too, favours waving, cheering at the top of their voices for him to succeed. They should have been here with him; both were taken far too soon. His victory, if he gains it today, will not be whole without them. But he'll remember them every day for the rest of his rule. His brothers even, grievances forgotten, flank him in his charge. This is for them too, after all. Tudor is an enemy of them all, not just Richard.

With their encouragement in mind, he spurs his horse harder, as they approach their target.

He nearly makes it.

As his force engages with Tudor's, Richard makes sure his sword takes its fair share of blood, not leaving his men to do all the work: never let anyone say he was a coward on the field. Not today of all days. He topples the Tudor banner himself, cutting down the bearer, Sir William Brandon. He glimpses the fear on Tudor's face, before turning again, to kill one, two, three other, nameless, men. Then he unhorses the traitor Sir John Cheyne. That feels good, for a heartbeat – personal revenge on one who stood so firmly with the York brothers for so long, only to switch allegiance to Tudor. He's unlikely to die, but it gives Richard a burst of strength, tempered when he sees Sir James Harrington fall, and one of his oldest friends, Richard Ratcliffe. The aftermath of this battle, even if won, will hurt.

It's all going to plan.

Until it isn't.

When the fall happens, it happens quickly. Too quickly. Richard hardly perceives the chain of events. First, the smallest of tragedies. The falling blow of a halberd, a damaged helmet, and the choice of removing his protection or fighting blind. No choice at all. In a heartbeat, another strike from a halberd, and he's off his horse, on the ground – by now little more than mud.

Richard is down, but not yet defeated.

But then everything begins to blur.

The spirits he rode with are fading away, friends replaced by foes, both in his mind and in his vision, all-too-good now his helmet has vanished, lost somewhere in the chaos. He'd reach out to his retainers, but there's too much confusion. Somebody, from somewhere, offers him a horse, but it's too late surely? There's no room to mount as his enemies close in, weapons drawn. He feels the blades find their way through his armour, loosening now he's fighting on his feet, sword swinging. He refuses the horse, fights on as best he can, but then the blows strike harder. The hilt of a sword catches him full-force in the face. He stumbles back, almost loses his footing. His feet struggle to find purchase in the mud. Then he realizes to his horror that what he balances himself against is his squire, dying on his knees at Richard's feet.

No time for sorrow. Richard turns again, sword arm raised again. Blocks again, hits again, blocks again, hits again, blocks, until … The pain is so sudden, so strong. It lasts only a moment. No time to fully grasp what's happened. Sights and sounds of the field fade in that instant.

He didn't make it. His blood on the ground, not Tudor's. His life lost. His crown forfeit.

As he falls, Richard remembers his words at the start of all this.

'God forbid that I retreat one step. I will either win the battle as a king, or die as one.'

And he did. Die as a king. Nobly and with honour, doing everything a king should do. Being everything a king should be. Even his enemies had to admit that truth.

'God forbid that I retreat one step. I will either win the battle as a king, or die as one.'
(The reported last words of King Richard III)

> *'... like a spirited and most courageous prince, Richard fell in battle on the field and not in flight.'*
> *(Crowland Chronicles, 1485–6)*

> *'He bore himself like a noble soldier and ... honourably defended himself to his last breath.'*
> *(John Rous, pre-1491)*

About the author

Jennifer C. Wilson has been stalking dead monarchs since childhood, but now, happily, it tends to result in a story... Moving back to her native north-east after university, she took creative writing courses in evening classes and hasn't looked back. She won North Tyneside Libraries' Story Tyne short story competition in 2014, and her debut novel (*Kindred Spirits: Tower of London*) was published in 2015. Since then, she has written a range of historical and contemporary tales, including expanding the Kindred Spirits series, with Richard III as her regular leading man (albeit in ghostly form!).

Jennifer also runs North Tyneside Writers' Circle, established in 2017, and has written two non-fiction books, based on these and other workshops.

Website: https://jennifercwilsonwriter.wordpress.com/
Twitter: https://x.com/inkjunkie1984

Have you found a new favourite author within these pages?

Most of the authors featured in *A Spirited and Most Courageous Prince* have written full-length novels (and in some cases non-fiction books) about King Richard and his times that you may enjoy. Why not check them out? Details can be found by following the links in each author's biographical note at the end of their story.

Some authors have also contributed stories to the previous Ricardian anthologies, *Grant Me the Carving of My Name* and *Right Trusty and Well Beloved...*, both edited by Alex Marchant, and two other collections, *The Road Not Travelled: Alternative Tales of the Wars of the Roses*, edited by Joanne R. Larner, and *Yorkist Stories: A Collection of Short Stories about the Wars of the Roses*, edited by Michèle Schindler. Proceeds from all four books are donated to charity – the first three to Scoliosis Support and Research (formerly SAUK) and the fourth to Médecins Sans Frontières.

Also available:

Grant Me the Carving of My Name

and

Right Trusty and Well Beloved…

Two anthologies of short fiction (and poetry) inspired by King Richard III, also sold in support of Scoliosis Support and Research (formerly Scoliosis Association UK, SAUK). Both can be bought from Amazon via mybook.to/GrantMetheCarving and mybook.to/RightTrusty or direct from Alex Marchant – AlexMarchant84@gmail.com

Praise on Amazon for *Right Trusty and Well Beloved…*

'A fabulous collection.'

'Pure bliss … I could not put the book down.'

'Another nice mix of Ricardian fiction … something to appeal to all tastes.'

'So beautifully and hauntingly written.'

'An excellent and entertaining series of short stories and poems. Some are exciting, some amusing, some tragic and will make you cry.'

'Another collection of tales, looking at the myths and realities of Richard III … all well written and worth reading, and help to redress the traditional image of Richard with fact based and more credible narratives.'

Printed in Great Britain
by Amazon